D1517619

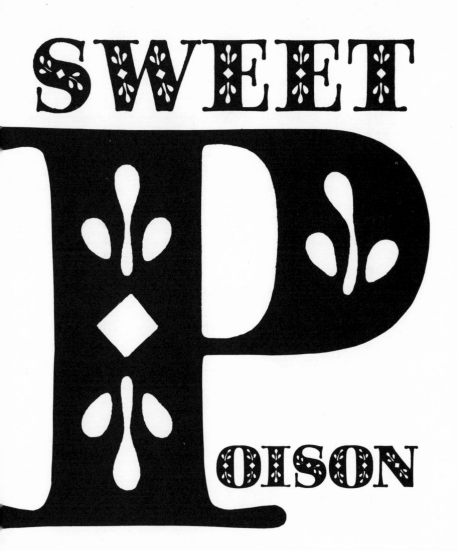

SWEET POISON

Translated by David Lobdell

Two Novels by Pierre Turgeon

COMING SOON

For Emmanuelle

SWEET POISON

PART ONE: INCUBATION

THE PRACTICE OF CRUELTY

I don't know during what era it was that that Norman whose
blood still flows in my veins embarked for New France, but
my grandfather's prominent brow, hard narrow eyes and thick
neck were clearly inherited from that race of conquerors who
in coming to the New World had bitten off more than they
could chew, seeing it only as a means of self-enrichment. Mo-
tivated in turn by self-interest, Vincent married the daughter
of a launderer, a nervous, whimsical, extravagant woman
whose name was Suzanne. A common love of lucre and the
children born to them each year for more than a decade lent
an air of stability to that union of perpetual quarrels and
infidelities.

At six o'clock every morning, my grandmother would fill
her big tumbler with laundry, clothes so filthy and greasy they
were not fit to be handled without tongs. Then she would
open the steam valves leading to the manglers and ticket the
clothes that had been laundered the previous day. At seven
o'clock, her employees would enter the soot-blackened building, where, in an atmosphere of insufferable heat, they would
work without a break, amidst the gasping wheezes of machinery and the acidic odours of detergent. These girls hailed
from Saint-Malo, the poor quarter of Quebec. Lacking background, education and physical beauty, they lived in constant
fear of Suzanne, an Amazon who was intimately familiar with
their fornications and who wouldn't hesitate at blackmail if
they failed to clean their quota of shirts, a number that was
posted daily on a large leather board and that varied with the
affluence of the customers and my grandmother's fluctuating
moods. By dint of nagging, yelling and scheming, my grandmother watched her business grow, as the branch stores and
delivery trucks multiplied. But, despite her fortune, she never

succeeded in infiltrating the upper echelons of society, which looked upon her as a parvenue, a daughter of the lower classes intoxicated with overnight success. I was familiar with those mansions, with their multiple gables and garrets, where voices were muffled between thick walls and only a pale, sickly light filtered through the blinds and the heavy damask drapes; mansions inhabited by all the magpies, nitwits and dupes who comprised the aristocracy of Quebec: notaries, doctors, lawyers, faithful apostles of the status quo, sleepwalking their way through life and preaching submission to the masses, reeking of furniture polish, napthaline and the confessional. I was sufficiently familiar with them to appreciate how they must scorn the petulance of a woman like my grandmother, bundled up in her extravagant fur coats and her bell-shaped hats with the long red feathers, perfumed, beribboned, talking loudly and crudely, sinking her fangs into the priest and any other man who did not meet with her immediate approval. Shortly before the war, vexed at having reached the age of 40, she took herself off to play the tourist in Europe and Asia, an excursion that was underwritten by 50 hired hands and ransomed by nine brats who had been packed off to boarding-schools. When my father enlisted in the Air Force, it was to escape the insipid meals, the clappers and the switches of the nuns. Of his mother, he recalled only the yells and the maledictions. That versatile woman, who had never wasted any love on her children, would later counsel my mother to have an abortion, to be unfaithful to Edouard.

I have a photo in my room of my father in his aviator's uniform: the tight, curly hair, the gentle eyes, the mouth twisted into a half-smile. Neither his cap, worn smartly on the right side of his head, nor his bomber jacket, with its unfringed epaulettes, eclipse the almost feminine allure of those smooth cheeks and glossy pink lips, slightly parted in an expression of apparent pleasure, revealing two upper incisors.

Returning from leave in the city, Edouard showed his pass to the guard, who silently opened the gate. An asphalt road ran between the log barracks, stretching all the way to the landing field with its strings of red and blue lights. There was a low, snarling sound, which accelerated and became a roar, and the squat, black silhouette of a Lancaster rolled heavily toward the end of the runway. Edouard clenched his jaws. He would never pilot a plane. When the instructor flashed the picture of a Messerschmitt or a Junker on the screen, he could identify it at once; and he had passed all the physical tests. But he had failed his exams in theory, being insufficiently familiar with the English language. When he had protested, his teacher had gazed scornfully at him and asked:

"But why are you French?"

Soon, the entire camp had taken up this cynical retort, using it as an irrefutable argument whenever the handful of French Canadians in the squad deigned to register a complaint. Because of his excellent eyesight and quick reflexes, Edouard had been assigned the dangerous position of tail-gunner.

He was watching the Lancaster take off when three men surged out of the shadows and surrounded him. A scrawny fellow with a Bourbon nose sneered:

"You stupid Frenchman, what ..."

A blow to the Adam's apple cut the man short, as he doubled up with a moan. Edouard ducked the hook of a fat sergeant, sinking the toe of his boot into the man's gut. There remained only the third assailant, who stood before him gasping for breath, his face beaded with sweat, a knife clutched in one hand.

"He's scared to death," thought Edouard.

And, picking up his cap, he went slowly on his way. But at the sound of a step behind him on the gravel, he whirled about, arms and legs spread wide, fearing the third man was about to leap on him. An officer stood in the middle of the road, his switch tucked beneath his arm.

"Come here, Frenchie!" he yelled.

9

The man with the knife had vanished. The captain must have seen him.

"So you're a tough guy, eh?" he said to Edouard, who stood at attention before him.

The other two men got slowly to their feet. In the distance, there was the whining sound of an engine.

"Spitfire," thought my father automatically.

He was sentenced to ten days' fatigue duty and solitary confinement. The task he was assigned was to polish the floor of the latrine. Each time it was sparkling, a sergeant passed by and "accidentally" upset a pail of dirty water over it. Edouard went back to his work in silence, though once he hammered the walls in his rage. One evening, the soldier who handed him his plate of beans said in an undertone:

"You'd better watch it when you get out."

In this way, they continued to provoke him. And if he made a move to defend himself, he was sent back to the pound. The insults and the persecutions did not humiliate him, however; they were to be expected between enemy races. He was much more suspicious of the English who made an effort to meet him half way, who showed a certain sympathy for their French-speaking compatriots.

Suddenly, the snow began to dance in the light that streamed from the windows and that transformed the yard into a giant black-and-white chequer-board. Intoxicated with joy, Edouard pressed his face between the bars, opened the window and inhaled the icy air that even bore the smell of freedom. Memories of his childhood with the nuns, whose rapacious nails had lacerated him even in his dreams, caused him momentarily to choke up; but the sight of the falling snow quickly effaced all recollections of the frightful emptiness of the past, like an unexpected boon from heaven.

"Close the window," whimpered a little Jew, who had been locked up for desertion. "I'm cold."

Edouard scooped up a handful of melting snow from the window-sill and rubbed it over his face. His mind was made up: the moment he was released, he would head straight for Quebec.

"Go to hell!" he replied to the little Jew, whose teeth were chattering.

Disembarking from the train, Edouard hailed a cab and gave the driver his parents' address. The snow-covered city resembled a cream cake: the streets were streams of chocolate and the nordic sun sitting low in the sky was sprinkled with icing sugar. Dressed in civvies, Edouard devoured the caramel and pistachio houses with his eyes. Then he recognized the family home, a loaf of spice bread bathed in a sweet, mellow light. But when he stepped out of the old, rust-coloured Packard, the spell was suddenly broken: the cold air whipped at him and the setting suddenly became hard, clear, keen. The few pedestrians hastened toward the warmth of their homes with the alacrity of trout in an icy stream. Then the thin, angular figure of Suzanne appeared in a glass doorway. She was wearing a loose black dress with gold trim. For an instant, the eyes of mother and son met. Did he only imagine it or was that a witch gazing at him, one of the ugly hags that had peopled his childhood picture-books? It was probably only the play of the light, deflected by the net curtains. The vision vanished. Had it not been for the fluttering of the curtains, Edouard would have sworn that he'd been the victim of an hallucination.

He stepped into the vestibule, where two mirrors hanging face-to-face reflected his image into infinity. He began to climb the spiral staircase leading to his room on the upper floor, paying no heed to the shouts and curses emanating from various corners of the house. Suddenly, a giant with a porcine face and small piercing eyes blocked his way, gripping both wrought-iron railings.

"'Ti-coune!" the giant exclaimed with delight. "Hey, guys, 'Ti-coune's back!"

The doors on the ground floor opened to disgorge an assortment of strange characters. Edouard lowered himself onto a step and sat contemplating his brothers grouped below him in the huge living-room. There were twelve of them, all reeking of tobacco, beer and urine, all endowed with the same square-set shoulders and the same small grey eyes. Edouard hated every last one of them.

"Where's Louis?" he asked.

"Dead of lung cancer," replied one of the brothers, smiling like a ferret.

"How did the old lady take it?"

"Oh, you know her," muttered the colossus behind him.

"And the old man?"

A few heads turned in the direction of an old man who sat reading in an armchair, his head wreathed in a cloud of pipe smoke.

"Papa!" shouted one of the boys. "Ti-coune's come back with the Victoria Cross!"

There were sporadic bursts of laughter as Vincent Quillevic raised his lifeless eyes in Edouard's direction and spat into a large copper spittoon. Then, all that could be heard was the ticking of a grandfather clock as the group silently dispersed. Edouard picked up his bag and followed his brother up the stairway, his feet sinking into the deep, cream-coloured carpet.

"Armand, where can I find the old lady at this hour?" he asked.

"Why? You want to put the touch on her? It won't work, you know, she's too tight."

"I just want to talk to her about Christine," said Edouard, opening the door to his room.

"Why? You knock her up?" asked Armand, a twinkle in his eye.

Edouard seized him by the throat.

"Don't you ever say that again, you bastard!"

"I don't understand you, 'Ti-coune," Armand said, shaking his head in bewilderment as he moved down the hallway.

Edouard dumped the contents of his bag on the bed,

splashed water over his face in the little basin, placed a record by Caruso on the gramophone and stretched out on top of his clothing.

The following morning, he was awakened with a start by a strange sound. A large, sleek rat was curled up on the bed, staring at him out of red, incandescent eyes, looking evil enough to eat a child. My father threatened it with his pillow, and it leapt from the bed and darted behind an *armoire*. Somewhere, a vacuum cleaner hummed its mournful tune. Edouard pulled himself to his feet. Outside, a patrol car passed the house so slowly he thought it was going to stop. Slipping into his jacket, he thought: "I can't stay here, the MPs will be looking for me, they'll question the neighbours."

In the kitchen, he absent-mindedly greeted the maid and a number of strangers, probably friends of his brothers. He gulped down two peanut-butter tarts, then stepped into the yard, where 50-odd blue-and-white delivery vans stood parked. Suddenly, a swarm of uniformed drivers emerged from the large building next door and climbed into the vehicles. An alarm sounded eight o'clock. Edouard entered the building, where long rows of verdigris metal eggs stretched into the distance, humming and vibrating like wasps. Jets of steam hissed in the semi-darkness, while the employees piled the dirty laundry into tumblers, then slammed the glass doors. Agitated by the rotating movements of the machines, the clothes looked like streams of black seaweed, the medley of colours and fabrics giving birth to strange landscapes, dreamlike figures......

Standing beside a mangler, Suzanne was bawling out a teenage girl who had singed a petticoat. Edouard asked her if he could speak with her. She hustled him toward a soundproof office.

"What do you want, 'Ti-coune?" she asked, standing with her hands on her hips, her thighs quivering impatiently.

"I've deserted, I need a place to hide out."

"Go to hell!"

13

Edouard seized her wrists and muttered:

"You've got to help me."

She seized a ring of keys from the desk and tossed it at him.

"I evicted one of my tenants on Rue Saint-Jacques."

Edouard left, and she stood for a moment, sucking her arm where her son's fingers had left four red crescents.

Outside the movie house, people were jostling one another, treading the blackened snow right into the foyer. Amongst them were respectable citizens, looking stiff in their long black coats and glaring at the young ruffians who slapped their dates on the rump; civil servants, with sheepish looks on their faces, as if they had just emerged from a brothel; military personnel on leave, their eyes lighting up at the sight of the pretty usherettes in their bright red uniforms. . . . There was already a line-up for the last show. Car doors opened to swallow up women huddled against the cold.

Edouard took Christine by the arm and broke into a run, propelled by the gusts of wind that lifted the tails of his coat. Here and there, streetlamps probed the darkness, the snow clinging to them like lunar foliage. At the end of the street, framed by its heavy walls, stood the Porte Saint-Denis. A cluster of silent commuters huddled beneath the arch, waiting for a trolley-car.

"You're a strange guy," gasped Christine, out of breath from running. "Why go alone to the club, when we could join the rest of the gang?"

"I told you, I don't like crowds."

Before them hung a red and yellow sign, glazed with ice, bearing the inscription: AU CARTIER LATIN, in medieval script. Edouard pulled open the door with its wrought-iron grating. Inside, a few customers sat scattered about the walls of the room, which were decorated with bevelled mirrors and ornamental bric-a-brac. My father and Christine took seats at a table.

"A real hermit, that's what you are!" she joked, ruffling

14

Edouard's hair. "A real St. John the Baptist! You even have the curly hair for the role. Well, what are we going to wet our lips on to pass the time?"

Edouard ordered two beers.

"Now, tell me how you managed to get this leave," said Christine, lighting a cigarette. "You said in your letters it would be impossible."

"I've deserted. But not out of cowardice. I enjoy killing— too much!"

"Is that why you deserted?"

"It's one of the reasons."

He sat gazing at his big hands, which lay flat on the white metal table-top.

"When I was a kid, they beat us and mocked us, as a matter of course. They did everything in their power to corrupt us. 'Yes, sister.' 'Thank you, sister.' Then, there comes a day when you've had enough of grovelling and turning the other cheek. You learn to be hard, just like them. The walls that were closing in on you suddenly crumble."

The waiter brought them their beers. A pop tune was playing faintly on the radio. The lower part of her face hidden by her glass, Christine sat gazing at Edouard with a mixture of uneasiness and curiosity.

"Cruelty," he went on, "requires a long apprenticeship. First, you have to learn to hate your own body. You smash the mirrors, those ancient symbols of man's narcissism. Then you take a sliver of glass and mutilate yourself. When you've taught yourself to hate everything about yourself, when you've become your own worst enemy, you stop feeling pity for anything or anyone. Hitler must be like that."

He signalled the waiter for another beer.

"The next step," he continued, "is to seize a spike and drive it into your enemy's head. You watch as a mucous-coloured jelly comes trickling out. In the folds and swellings of that disabled brain swarm all the thoughts that conspired against you. You set fire to all that vermin. And, in doing so, you break the last of your chains. Today, we must either forget all the old notions of right and wrong, or go under. No pity for the weak or the helpless. Tenderness, charity, forgiveness: these things only serve to poison our existence."

"And what did this enemy do to you?"

"She gave me life."

"Your mother!" exclaimed Christine.

"Yes, but I don't expect you to understand that. She has only one ambition: to destroy us, her sons. And I'm not sure she won't succeed."

"With so much hatred in you, how can you possibly love me?"

He stroked her hands with an almost maniacal fervour.

"I don't know, you're the miracle. To reach the dawn, we have to pass through the night. Perhaps love is hiding at the end of the tunnel. Once all the vermin are burned . . . Oh God, I rack my brains! There are so many things I want to tell you. You're as pretty as a freshly-laundered skirt . . . and your eyes are as deep as a soap vat . . . and your thighs—oh, pardon me, you're a respectable young woman, you're not the neighbourhood tart—but your skin, your skin is as soft as a chair after a long day's work, and your waist is as slender as a coat hanger, and your hair is as glossy as starch . . . and your lips, oh! your lips are as hot as an iron!"

She broke into laughter, flushed with delight.

"You've drunk too much, my little laundryman!"

A gang of young ruffians suddenly burst into the place, pushing and shouting. A pimply-faced adolescent exclaimed:

"Edouard Quillevic! What a surprise! And what is the ace of the invincible Royal Air Force doing here in Quebec?"

My father's lips curled into a sneer.

"Are you coming?" he asked, shaking off the intruder, who had seized his arm. "There's a bad smell in here."

"Where are we going?" asked Christine, pulling on her coat.

"My mother gave me the keys to one of her flats. I'm going

to hide out there till I can find something better."

As they were leaving, a voice on the radio announced that the Sixth Army of General Von Paulus had encircled Stalingrad.

"They've been saying the same thing for four months now," muttered Edouard with a shrug.

Outside, the cold air struck them like a wall of fire, entering their mouths and stinging their gums. They took a taxi to a two-storey tenement, flanked on one side by a snack bar and, on the other, by a vacant lot with a Coca-Cola billboard standing in it. They climbed a rickety staircase and made their way down a long hallway full of tenants engaged in a nocturnal row.

"We've got a right to have a bit of fun!" screeched a young woman in rags at a skinny man who was threatening to strike her.

The lovers entered the apartment, which reeked of tobacco and sweat. On the coffee-table lay a pipe, a pack of filthy playing-cards and two unmatching candles. Prints of diving aircraft hung on the walls. They lowered themselves onto the sofa-bed. The eyes that my mother turned lovingly upon Edouard were a vivid, sparkling blue. He felt his heart leap. He drew her to him, kissed her, devoured her with his caresses. They were just beginning to feel the warmth return to their bodies, when they were startled by a loud knocking that resounded throughout the house. The tenants in the hallway had suddenly fallen silent. Another series of violent blows shook the door. Seizing a steel pipe, which he concealed behind his back, Edouard went to answer.

In the doorway stood Suzanne, looking stiff and austere in a long black coat. Behind her were several policemen. Pointing at her son, she said:

"There's my cowardly deserter of a son. Take him and lock him up. I've done my duty as a mother and a citizen."

She bowed curtly, then, casting a scornful glance at Christine, who was confusedly trying to smooth her rumpled skirt, turned and left. Edouard was already being hustled out of the building, having relinquished his weapon with a sob. In the street, his shoes filled up with snow. Before he was propelled head-first into the patrol car, he turned and saw Christine standing stiffly in the doorway, her hair wildly dishevelled. She called to him:

"I love you."

For a moment, the pulsing red lights of the police cars cast a crimson glow over the façades of the buildings and the sirens wailed like a pack of hungry wolves; then the vehicles passed into the night. Sensing that she was being watched, Christine turned and saw Suzanne standing inside the snack bar, her nose pressed to the window. Her mouth was twisted into a sneer. Because the lower part of her body was concealed by a blackboard containing the menu of the day, only her head was visible: she bore an uncanny resemblance to a reptile.

"The enemy," thought Christine and returned inside for her coat, which she'd left on the bed.

THE CAVALIER IN THE TRICORN

Edouard was condemned to rot for six months in a military prison. He slept on the floor, his naked body wrapped in a blanket. He was awakened at dawn and spent his days breaking stones along the roadside. In his letters to Christine, he restricted himself to generalities. She consoled him with the promise of her love, and rejoiced that he was safe, far from the fighting. Despite the rationing of gasoline, her father was chauffeured about in a limousine belonging to the organization of which he was the director. Occasionally, she managed to persuade him to let her be driven to the camp where Edouard was being held prisoner.

An enclosure of dark red bricks surrounded the penitentiary, whose walls cowered below the windswept sky. A few clumps of weeds sprouted amongst the uneven flagstones in the courtyard.

"I won't be long, Alphonse," said Christine to the uniformed chauffeur who held the door open for her.

Wire partitions glistened with beads of moisture. Pale lightbulbs illuminating endless corridors. She was shown into a room whose floor had been freshly waxed. Steel beams crisscrossed the ceiling. The wan light, the bare, windowless walls: these things made her feel as if she was in an underground city, where she found it hard to breathe. Even the most familiar sounds took on a strange, ominous note.

She was left alone. Suddenly, she felt embarrassed by her appearance: that candy-striped, silk dress! She wanted to appear simple, like the sentiments that inflated her heart. A steel door slammed behind her. Looking truculent in his striped uniform, Edouard stood before her, his cap in his hands. His fingernails were black.

"I can't get you out of my thoughts," she said. "They laugh at me at home, because your name is always on my lips."

"How's your friend, Pascal?"

"I don't see him anymore."

She blushed at the lie, discovering in Edouard's dark eyes and square jaw a violence that had hitherto been concealed by his timidity.

As if in a trance, he muttered: "One day, soon, you'll receive an invitation to attend a ball at my palace. The entire city will be there. The champagne will flow. . . . Do you have a cigarette?"

She kept an eye on the clock: only three minutes left.

Throwing his head in the air, he said: "My father is well off. One of his sons just got married and already he's making a bundle from the laundry. My wife," he went on, sucking the smoke deep into his lungs, "will be like you: attractive, sensible, sober . . . and I'm not such a bad devil, you know."

The key grated in the lock. A guard commanded my father to follow him.

"Will you marry me, miss?"

19

"Of course I will. And you don't have to be so formal with me, you know. After all, we're not strangers."

"What about your parents?"

"I'll convince them. At any rate, I'm of age now."

Back in the car, passing through wheatfields flattened by the wind, Christine opened the glass partition separating her from the chauffeur.

"Alphonse, I'm so happy!" she exclaimed.

Guillaume Séchaud flatly refused to allow his daughter to marry a deserter. Suspicious of the lofty airs assumed by Edouard's family, he hired a private detective, who, after several weeks of snooping, exposed the hypocrisy of all this high living. It seemed the Quillevics were deeply in debt; not only that, but, with the collaboration of a few influential civil servants, they cheated regularly on their taxes. Following his release, Edouard endured the snubs of his future parents-in-law, who sometimes kept him cooling his heels for hours at a time only to inform him that Christine was out.

They met on the sly, taking long walks in the park, where they lay side by side on mounds of dead leaves, their eyes fixed upon the clouds that hung motionless above the cliff; or huddled together in the underbrush of the Plains of Abraham, speaking quietly of the children that would one day be theirs. One evening, they found themselves climbing a narrow street littered with horse droppings and lined with big houses with mansard windows. In the yards, children were squabbling like sparrows over a breadcrust. A pale, thin young man with a lock of hair hanging over his brow stood on a street corner, singing a lament, while a little blond girl moved amongst the spectators, shaking a metal cup with a few coins in it. Hand-in-hand, the lovers turned into a steep alley leading to the upper town. The yellow orb of the setting sun looked as if it were resting on the pavement; this, and the sounds of a hammer beating on an anvil, with its limpid evocation of an earlier age, allowed Christine to believe that a cavalier in a tricorn and a sky-blue frock coat might at any moment come galloping through the gateway with its fleur-de-lis coat-of-arms. Rejuvenated by love, the world seemed to be flickering to life after a long, troubled sleep.

Christine often brooded over these brief moments of joy in their lives, convinced that they augured well for the future. One evening, climbing onto a bus, Edouard openly rebuked two bums for their blasphemous tongues. Then, pale with rage, he lowered himself into a seat.

"Those impious louts should be horse-whipped!"

At the sight of his dark gaze and trembling lips, Christine was afraid to chide him, for fear he might break into tears.

On the other hand, whenever they attended house parties or joined in communal outings in the country, he was an endless source of witticisms and jokes. Assuming the droll air of a king's jester, he could tell stories in such a way as to bring out the ridiculous side of things:

"After we'd spent the whole day carrying wood, the nuns drew lots for a piece of candy. And who do you think was the winner? Arthur, a lazy devil whose drawers were filled with caramels and chocolates and who was as fat as a whale! I'd done the work of four, and what did I get for all my pains? A slap on each cheek for crying 'Unfair!'"

He bought a camera. My mother served as his model. In some shots, she is wearing a black suit buttoned up to the neck and a hat with a small veil. In others, she is lying on an old-fashioned canopy bed in flimsy underclothing.

Meanwhile, Suzanne had returned from the island of Bali, to which she had been drawn from her reading of a popular novel. While she emptied her bags of their cargo of cheap jewellery, Buddha statuettes and multicoloured fabrics, her housemaid chattered away as she stowed the henceforth-useless flowered jackets and sandals in the closet.

"Your husband spends all his time dozing in that old easy chair of his, with his eternal pipe in his mouth. Shall I have this ermine put in storage, Suzanne? And your boys are full of the devil! Their friends come right in without knocking and sprawl about in the living-room; they threaten to tear the place apart if they aren't offered a drink."

She dropped to her knees to lay a polka-dot bolero in the bottom of a box. Struggling back to her feet, clutching a handful of mothballs, she went on:

"As for that rascal, Edouard, he's been hanging out with Christine Séchaud. And he's sleeping with her too, if you want my opinion."

"Her father is rich, isn't he?" asked Suzanne.

"He sure is! But he's decided to be difficult. He won't hear of your son marrying into his family."

Suzanne lit a cigarette and slipped into a dressing-gown.

"Lay out a dress for me," she said. "I'm going out. I'll show that snob, Séchaud, who he's dealing with."

A MAN OF STRAW

My maternal grandfather, Guillaume Séchaud, was born 1 January, 1889, in a poor quarter of Montreal. From his father, Aristide, he learned the ancient skills of carpentry. In his workshop, the saw and plane and hammer squealed and squeaked and rang out all day long. The pungent odour of glue got into everything, even the petticoats of his wife.

In the evenings, after dinner, the old folks would talk of the years of the Long Darkness and tell tales of predatory were-wolves.

"You're making that up, Grandpa!" Aristide would reply, crossing himself.

A large black crucifix, with several dusty palm fronds interlaced beneath it, hung on the plaster wall. The wife and child went to bed, while the men sat on, drinking and uttering bold oaths.

One day, Aristide was brought home bleeding to death. During a hunting trip, his father-in-law had lodged a bullet in his right shoulder. They laid him out on a table. Since he refused to let them amputate the arm, the gangrene eventually reached his heart and Aristide departed for the land of the moles.

The widow and son were taken in by a great-aunt, a prudish old woman who put Guillaume to work delivering the robes and cassocks she sewed and mended. He knocked on the doors of houses before which horse-drawn carriages stood; hat in hand, he entered salons set ablaze by glittering chandeliers and dropped to his knees to arrange the robes of smooth-cheeked, sweet-smelling magistrates. When classes resumed, his Great Aunt Emilie undressed him, tossed him into a tub of hot water and scrubbed him down with a stiff brush and a cake of black soap. When he was primped and polished and decked out in his Sunday best, he was sent off to beg for school-books at the homes of bigots who had already been catechized in his favour by the local priest. When he was fourteen, Emilie felt his muscles and sent him to work on the docks. His education had been limited to a smattering of grammar and arithmetic. But with his first glimpse of wealth, Guill-aume had acquired a taste for better things. Seated on a moor-ing post, hypnotized by the river, the bellowing of ships' horns and the throngs of passengers embarking for Europe, he devoured his lunch and silently repeated his grandfather's words:

"You are noble, not in rank but in character. This is a base world, which often counts for nothing. But I foresee great things for you."

From unloading ships, he acquired a pair of powerful bi-ceps. Beneath the shock of red hair, his pale blue eyes inso-lently ogled the beribboned ladies. At the sight of the young lads, looking distinctly uncomfortable in their top hats and black frock-coats, hurrying along at the side of workers who slapped their thighs and shouted obscenities at them, he won-dered at the cowardice of the latter, too intimidated to lash out at their feeble exploiters.

Saturday evenings were spent with friends on a terrace overlooking the river, with its long rows of concessions and its garlands of coloured paper flowers strung between the lamp-posts. When night fell, Chinese lanterns cast yellow and blue reflections over the laughing faces of the girls, who sauntered along, swinging their hips. In the music-halls, orchestras beat out the rhythms of the can-can, while the dancers hitched up their skirts to the clamorous cries of the spectators. The beer flowed freely, adding to the heaviness of the already smoky atmosphere, faces sparkled, exhausted bodies sprawled in chairs and on benches. It was on one of these festive evenings that Guillaume met Madeleine, who worked in a cotton mill. Small and buxom, she rolled her brown eyes seductively at him, her eyebrows like two little circumflexes pasted to her brow. Though she let herself be kissed after the dancing was over, she drew the line when Guillaume tried to pull her down on top of him in the middle of a vacant lot.

The stevedore dreamed of having a home of his own, his mother and his great-aunt having become almost impossible to live with. The former, as the result of a fall from a balcony, suffered from uraemia and carried the unpleasant odour of her ailment about with her; while the latter, almost a hundred years old, was so bloated from dropsy she could actually see her reflection in her own hands. As for Guillaume's sister, Louise, she had been diagnosed as consumptive and spent her days lying on a cot, facing a window through which filtered a pale light. It was Guillaume who did the sewing, the washing, the cooking, to the incessant complaints of the three invalids who disputed his attention like furies. To get away from it all, he locked himself into a small room, where, by the light of a candle, he read aloud in a hesitant voice. He was fascinated by electricity, which was just then beginning to replace gas in street lighting. With the aid of an English dictionary, he made his way painstakingly through a manual on the subject, then hired himself out as an apprentice to a master-electrician.

Madeleine's family lived in a gosling-green house sur-

24

rounded by a rickety fence. Hens foraged right up to the front door. A few chestnut trees languished in the dirt yard, concealing the outdoor latrine and a heap of rubble piled beneath the lean-to. The father, the former captain of a tug-boat, had been obliged by asthma to quit his work in the icy, fog-bound harbour. Now he spent his days hanging about the neighbourhood, flirting with the neighbours' wives and halfheartedly tending a kitchen garden. The mother, consumed with avarice and envy, plotted and schemed and made short-term loans at high interest rates. On pay days, she would sit wrapped up in a black shawl, watching the dusty road for signs of her sons on their weary way home from the mill. If, at the instigation of their comrades, they had spent too much at the tavern, she would deny them entry; the unfortunate creatures would have to sleep under the porch, awakening in the morning numb and feverish.

One evening, Guillaume invited Madeleine to the theatre. The cashier, the usherettes, the stage-manager, all greeted him as if he were an old friend. The play, entitled *L'Incendiare*, was about an insurrection instigated by a messianic revolutionary. After the final curtain, he turned to Madeleine and asked her if she had enjoyed it.

"Yes," she replied.

"I'm glad to hear it. I wrote it."

And hearing calls for the author, he climbed onto the stage, where, flushed with pleasure, he stood crushing his grey felt hat in his fingers.

Later, in the lounge, he spoke earnestly to Madeleine in his deep, ponderous voice, his elbows resting on the greasy table-top:

"For a long time, I was a fighter, without knowing what I was fighting for or against whom. I got into brawls with Irishmen, from which I emerged black-and-blue and invariably displeased with myself. Hurling bricks, breaking jaws, I ran up against the same injustices again and again, merely aggravating them with my violence. Gradually, I began to understand that I must fight, not with my fists but with this!"

And he struck his brow.

Madeleine peered at him, a little troubled by those thin lips and that slightly hooked nose. In the streetcar, he grew even more enthusiastic beneath the admiring gaze of his girl. If his half-digested readings on the International Workers' Brotherhood and the local syndicates had turned his head, he had used that head to formulate a simple plan for making his fortune. Many villages were still without electrical power stations. It was a question of getting there before anyone else.

"We'll show those big shots that French Canadians can do things for themselves!" he declared, oblivious to the fact that his companion was having trouble stepping down from the tram in her tight skirt.

When he entered the hovel where he lived, the noxious odour emanating from his mother's corner of the house turned his stomach. He threw himself onto his cot and gnawed his fists till they bled.

Sunday morning, Madeleine was up at dawn. After mass, which was celebrated by a young, sleepy-eyed priest, she killed a chicken, dressed it and spit it. Then, squatting on a little oak stool, she ground the coffee. Soon, the aroma of browning chicken awoke the other members of the family, who groaned blissfully beneath their covers.

That morning, the mother didn't go to church. Once the children were packed off to mass, she took a sack and placed the latest litter of kittens in it. Then she tossed it into her husband's lap.

"Go and drown them," she said.

He rose indolently, dragging the load over the flagstones and slamming the door behind him. Her face flushed from the heat of the burning logs, Madeleine dipped a ladle into the dripping-pan and basted the parson's nose, which was now a lovely golden hue. She didn't see her mother seize the leather strap. The first blow struck her on the nape of the neck, which her hair, twisted into a bun, did not protect. Then her assailant

26

began to strike her about the back and belly, screeching:

"You little slut! If you think I don't know about your shameless behaviour with that wretched Guillaume! You were carrying on right under my windows! You're going to confession, you strumpet!"

Madeleine, who at the first blow had collapsed on the floor, suddenly leapt to her feet. Her lips contorted into a grin, she tore the whip from her mother's hands and began to thrash the older woman with the calculated regularity of an automaton. The day she had been sold at the age of twelve to the owners of the textile mill; the day she had caught a glimpse of the gold pieces her parents kept hidden in a cashbox; the fancy-dress balls at which she had been obliged to make her appearance in rags—all these things returned to torment her now with the bitter taste of gall.

When her father returned, Madeleine was crouched on a chair, gazing dully at the burning chicken, while the sounds of her mother's sobbing could be heard from the bedroom.

"I haven't the heart to kill the poor creatures," muttered the man.

"I'll take care of it," replied his daughter.

And before continuing on her way to Guillaume's place, she stopped to listen to the wailing of the kittens tearing one another to pieces at the bottom of the well.

The Séchaud apartment was entered through a study, in which Guillaume often took refuge to escape the constant bickering in the household. This room and the kitchen, which looked out upon a yard filled with trashcans and litter, were at opposite ends of a long corridor, off which the bedrooms were reached, their badly fitting doors allowing a glimpse of unmade beds and dressers with peeling paint. Guillaume slept alone in the first room; the other was occupied by the three invalids.

As he was plunging a sheet into the washtub, Guillaume heard a light tap on the door, then Madeleine slipped into the room. Confused, he kicked aside the heap of dirty laundry, with its tell-tale signs of his family's wretchedness.

"How did you find me?" he asked.

"Through your friends."

And she told him she wanted to spend the next few days with him.

"Why don't we get married, then?"

"Why not?" she replied with a shrug.

"What's that strange woman doing here?" demanded a thin, sickly girl, drawing aside the bamboo curtain, her emaciated face and spindly legs evoking a whole lifetime of sadness and boredom. She had only a thread of a voice but it was fraught with anger, a state of mind accentuated by the raw-boned hands that gripped each other with a force that caused the knuckles to crack.

"It's my future wife," Guillaume replied.

And he turned his back on the intruder. When he and Madeleine were alone again, he explained:

"My sister, Louise. The doctors have given up hope for her. She's praying to Saint Joseph now for a miracle. She climbs the Oratory steps on her knees."

But, squatting on the floor, her eyes rolled back as if in ecstasy, Madeleine was washing the rags and did not reply.

The nights preceding her brother's wedding, Louise sat up late, listening for the slightest sound from Madeleine's room, fearful that the betrothed couple might try to make love on the sly. Meanwhile, Aunt Emilie and Madame Séchaud, looking like corpses, spent their time recounting their memories and bitterly complaining, showing no interest whatever in the living. Madeleine looked after them and cleaned up behind them, using her pay to brighten up the place with little objects of a simulated luxury: knick-knacks, lampshades of fluted cardboard, multicoloured wall hangings. The remainder of her savings she turned over to Guillaume, in the hope that he might increase it tenfold.

War broke out. On the front steps of the fire stations, the firemen sat knitting socks for the soldiers. Young people were stopped in the streets. During the searches, one of Madeleine's brothers hid in a corner behind the huge buffet. As the head of a household, Guillaume was exempt from conscription. Now in partnership with his former employer, he made huge profits from the munition-makers, who required more and more powerful sources of electrical energy. At the same time, he began to acquire the influence that he was to exercise over others and that would inspire his neighbours to greet him with the words: *"Bonjour, Monsieur Séchaud."* His grey cap was replaced by a bowler hat. At one point, a deal involving the purchase of high-tension wires took him to New York. Because he had driven over dirt roads and stopped several times to lubricate his car, he arrived at the hotel so filthy that the disgusted doorman refused him entry. On the return trip, he lost his way and fell in with a gang of smugglers, with whom he drank till dawn. Anything new fascinated him: 75 mm. cannons and chemical fertilizers, aviation and photography. He spent long hours trying to grasp the mysteries of the new technology, which he was resolved to master. The empty chit-chat of his loved ones held no interest for him. As for intellectuals, he was subject to the instinctive prejudice of the blue-collar worker for his white-collar brethren. His projects he allowed to brew in silence. The day the streetcar conductors rang their bells joyously and cried out: "The Germans have surrendered!" he was ready to make his move. Very stealthily, so as not to arouse suspicion, he set things in motion, importing large shipments of tools and transformers that he stored in a warehouse in the suburbs.

The deaths of his mother and great-aunt, who were both carried off in an epidemic of Spanish flu, held up his plans momentarily. Because of the odour, they were buried the very day of their deaths. Inconsolable, Louise retired to a convent, where a childhood friend awaited her. Now relieved of her duties toward her husband's family, Madeleine decided to have a child. Her husband observed the requisite period of mourning, then moved with his wife to Trois Rivières, where he was to supervise the construction of an electrical power plant.

Over the years, the river had eaten away at the mountainside, and now the water cascaded over the cliff, filling the air with an iridescent spray. Upstream of the falls, a bright red cubicle structure rose from the heaps of shale. Protected by tarpaulins, piles of construction materials were laid out in rows near a concrete dam. On a nearby promontory, a maze of black porcelain tubes and pipes whirred like grasshoppers. Trellised pylons stretched all the way to the horizon, their slender arms trembling beneath their heavy load of cables.

From the height of a glassed-in gallery, Guillaume surveyed the machine-room with its rumbling turbines and its snapping belts. His face was lined now and his body had grown a little thick. He was wearing a woollen vest as protection against the dampness. His hands cupped about his mouth, he shouted orders at a mechanic, then, consulting a pocketwatch, stepped out onto a terrace and gazed in the direction of the chalky road that wound through the forest. A few minutes later, a limousine emerged from the spruce trees and drew silently to a halt before the front door. It was Etienne who emerged to open the car door. An elderly, pink-cheeked gentleman greeted him with a nod and preceded him into the plant. He looked the premises over, then followed his guide into an office.

"So Mister Fulton?" asked Guillaume.

"You're going to sell this outfit to us," said the visitor, speaking French with a pronounced English accent.

"But that's out of the question!"

"You realize, of course, that we can break you just like that!"

And he snapped his fingers.

"You'll have to carry me out of the place feet-first."

"Tut-tut," said the other. "I admire your tenacity. But you must move with the times, if not . . ."

That evening, Madeleine was entertaining a few ladies of

society. Aside from a valet, she had no servants; the plump woman who served tea had been engaged for the occasion. A pale young girl, with a pink ribbon in her black hair, curtsied and retired.

"Christine is very well mannered," clucked a matron.

"Thanks to the nuns," replied Madeleine.

Of all the guests, there was not one who was not striking for her ugliness. One dozed, her multiple chins cascading over the lace frill of her blouse; while, to veil a complexion ravaged by smallpox, another had plastered her cheeks with a foot of rouge. They lived on the better streets of town, spurning the lower classes (certain ingénues deigned to scorn the bourgeoisie, as if *they* didn't have their own better neighbourhoods), passing the time in calumny and good works. In the company of all these frights, Madeleine was possessed of an almost diabolical vigour and beauty. But, following Guillaume's advice, she played the role of the fool.

"You have to get them off guard," he had said, "if you want to cut their throats."

"Electricity costs you nothing!" exclaimed a matron as the lights were switched on.

Madeleine smiled vaguely, pushing back a lock of hair that had fallen over her temple.

"Is she demented?" asked the same voice.

"Deaf. Since the birth of her daughter, she can hear only with her right ear."

Distinguishing only a few words, Madeleine warmly agreed. The ladies almost split their sides laughing. Just at that moment, Guillaume entered.

"You must excuse me, ladies, if I take your hostess away from you. But duty calls."

He puffed on a cigar as the house emptied.

"Is your little boy feeling any better? Give my regards to the doctor."

"What a bunch of old hens!" he groaned, after bowing out the last of the lady dragons. Having no taste for tobacco, he stubbed out the Havana and said: "Fulton came by today. It seems he looks upon me as a competitor. I can't call his bluff, he's a very powerful man, it looks like I'm going to have to sell out ... unless the prime minister comes to my aid."

Before retiring for the night, he promised to consult a hearing specialist on Madeleine's behalf; if necessary, to buy her an ear trumpet. His affection for her dated from the birth of their daughter, Christine, whom he idolized. Together, they had made the grade. When Mme. Séchaud recalled the nights she had been obliged to sleep in the bathroom (there being no bed for the only girl in the family), her parents bending over her to console her, she looked upon Guillaume as her lucky star and yielded to him in everything, rarely making demands. Meanwhile, he called her his little bundle of joy. They savoured their good fortune with that easy conscience and plain dealing they manifested in their business affairs. Better educated and therefore more vulnerable than his wife, Guillaume sometimes got worked up over the idea of social justice; he preferred to put up with a man's laziness and dishonesty than to dismiss him.

Following a sleepless night, he headed for Quebec City, where he planned to appeal to his powerful protector. His nerves were on edge and he drove badly. At one point, he swerved without reason and ended up in the ditch. The door on his side of the car was jammed, so he had to climb through the window and crawl onto the hood of the vehicle. The fields were alive with chirring grasshoppers and lowing cattle..

He stretched out on the grass, a wheel of the car spinning idly in the air. The sky was filled with fleecy clouds. The wind whistled about the ruins of a stable. Words took shape in Guillaume's mind, words that would never cross his lips, dangerous words that spoke of love and death. His domain was that of the mute. Suddenly, he felt irritated by all those hills and trees that sank back into the silence, like crabs into the sand. Aware that he must look odd lying there like that, he rose quickly to his feet. In no time at all, he had donned a new mask, the one of a knight of industry. By the time his car was towed away, he had hit upon the price he would ask for his mill: a good round sum, as well as the directorship of the company for the Quebec region. He no longer deluded himself about obtaining the prime minister's aid: politicians are always on the side of the strong.

EXTRACT FROM A DAILY PAPER

"On 8 August, 1932, M. Guillaume Séchaud was named the Director-General of Sorel Power, a member company of the Trois Rivières consortium. For nearly a quarter-century, M. Séchaud has been the personification of the local boy who made good. There was much rejoicing at the announcement of this appointment."

LIKE THE EBB TIDE

Ambition having been the guiding force in his life, Guillaume was bored to death in the role of a civil servant. He rarely participated in social functions and reading put him to sleep. For diversion, he took up big-game hunting and spent hours recounting his memories to Christine. He was deeply attached to that child who smelled of lavender, that adolescent immersed in the novels of Victor Hugo, that young woman who was devoted to him heart and soul. Without her, his life would have seemed empty, meaningless. So when Suzanne returned from her travels and importuned him on Edouard's behalf, she was wasting her breath. She brandished photos of Christine half-naked; he seized them and tore them up, then showed the loud-mouthed go-between to the door. She'd neglected to bring up the key argument, which nonetheless insinuated itself into my grandfather's mind: since at any rate he had to marry off his daughter to someone, why not to some young incompetent who, lacking a trade and without a cent to his name, would be dependent upon his father-in-law, thus ensuring that Christine should remain subject to his authority. He didn't articulate these thoughts, but he had a presentiment of their validity. Little by little, therefore, he came to believe that he was setting his child free, doing her a favour, whereas in fact he was enslaving her and doing her the greatest disservice.

For appearances' sake, it was decided that Edouard should study photography. So, following the wedding celebrations, he and my mother were packed off to New York. On the station platform, Suzanne turned to a friend and declared:

"I sure pulled one over on that little Séchaud!"

When they came in sight of the famous skyscrapers rising into the sky, with their rows and rows of glittering windows, when they inhaled the mingled odours of the sea and the sewers, the lovers were exultant. This city would be their nest, their alcove, their little fun-fair!

Dick, the distant relative who had promised to put them up free of charge, lived in a ramshackle building at the end of a maze of alleyways. They had scarcely finished unpacking when he asked them for a month's rent in advance. Thus, they were reduced at the outset to penury. Because he had to travel a long way to school, Edouard left at dawn, when the garbagemen and the milkmen were filling the streets with their clamour. Christine awoke later, alone and shivering, chased the mice off the quilt, had breakfast in a nearby coffee-house, and spent the hours until sunset in a movie house in order to forget her hunger.

"When it comes to our love," she told Edouard, "I refuse to compromise. What does it matter that there are bugs, as long as we're free? I'd rather die than ask my father for money. If you show signs of weakness, I'll be here to lend you my support."

At the beach, one day, inspired by some crazy notion, my father sped to a florist's stall and returned with an armful of orchids, the most ruinous of flowers. Christine hurled the bouquet to the ground and stamped on it. Before the amused throng of bathers, Edouard burst into tears.

"Do you want to destroy me, too?" he said.

It didn't take her long to realize that she had married a weak man. She dreamed that night that he was crumbling into hundreds of little red bricks, the kind used by children to build doll houses. Alarmed by this omen, she sat down and wrote to her father.

In a large hotel in downtown Manhattan, Guillaume paced the floor of a room with imitation mahogany wainscoting and imitation gold trim. The sounds of blasting car horns rose from the street, amplified by the skyscrapers. The tips of his fingers itched, a sign in his case of nervousness. Finally, Christine appeared, her face hollow and emaciated, dark circles about her eyes. Her dress was wet beneath the armpits. He grew pale.

"What has that damned fool allowed you to come to?" he demanded.

Gripping the back of a large armchair and articulating each word carefully, she said:

"If you ever expect to see me again, you'll be careful of what you say. How dare you? A man who was disowned by his own mother, packed off to an orphanage before he could hardly walk, one of the most wretched creatures on the face of the earth—and with good reason, too, because he was never loved and deserves an apology for even having been brought into this world! Do you think I would ever betray such a man? Not on your life! If only because of the example you set me, because of what you taught me!"

"I didn't intend you to become a martyr. Or a nursemaid."

She wheeled about and opened the door.

"Come back," he said in a calmer voice. "I want to help you."

"It's money I need, not advice."

He took out a roll of bills and counted:

"One hundred, two hundred . . ."

Despite the rebuff he had sustained, he knew he was the victor, reminding himself that noble scenes often end in this way. They talked about this and that, like two expert fencers who, unable to score, have decided to lay down their arms, brought together by a mutual admiration of each other's skills.

"Do you remember when we used to go on trips together?" asked Christine. "I would sleep with my head on your shoulder. I can even remember the feel of your jacket. It left red marks on my cheek; it had a minty smell."

M. Séchaud fought back his tears. Suddenly, he felt a sharp pain in his chest and his heart began to beat erratically. He collapsed on the bed, his lips blue, his chest shaken with a series of raucous gasps. Christine rushed for the porter and sent him in search of a doctor. While awaiting his arrival, she paced the floor of the room, her arms hanging helplessly at her sides, her torment increased by the knowledge that there was nothing she could do. Her father's lips moved without uttering a sound, but she thought she could detect the words: "Go away, go away," repeated over and over.

Deciding he must be mortified by her presence at such a moment, she turned her back to gaze out the window at a lighted sign. Several minutes passed, then the springs of the bed squeaked and she heard Guillaume say:

"Excuse me, it was just a moment of dizziness. I feel much better already."

The doctor, a big devil in a soft hat, diagnosed a mild heart attack and prescribed complete rest. Guillaume shrugged and eased him out the door.

"I'll leave you to rest," said Christine.

"You're a good girl."

And to conjure away the unclean thing that still prowled about them in the room, he winked and gave her an impish smile.

Back in the street, Christine realized that she had hidden her pregnancy and her anguish from the one person who mattered most to her in the world and in whom henceforth it would be impossible to confide. All about her, people were jostling one another: paunchy black men with dreamy, cretinous looks on their faces; weasel-faced youths in leather jackets, their fists probably closed about knives; pear-shaped figures idly scratching their crotches . . . a great throng of humans swept along like offal in the sewer. The city itself, with its multifaceted eyes, its mandibles and its erect stinger, resembled a scorpion about to pounce upon all those larva-like creatures.

How can we resist all that, thought Christine, when we know that our very deaths will lubricate the mechanism? There's no way to dominate or vanquish it. The most we can do is to join the excitement, move with the flow. My father, the child I am carrying, myself—we're all moving toward the very point from which we came. We're going nowhere, we'll return like the ebb tide.

Our children shall bear the pain of our faults; our fathers have already avenged them—Joseph de Maistre.

BETWEEN THE ANVIL AND THE HAMMER

Tourists are drawn to certain streets in old Quebec City because of their French character. Enter a house in the quarter and you will find yourself admiring the spiral staircases, the thick walls that keep out the summer heat and the garret windows that look out upon the river and its steady stream of smoke-belching steamers. It was on the ground floor of one of these historic structures, in the year 1946, that Edouard opened a photographic studio, attempting to lure passers-by with a window display of some of his better shots. The living-room he transformed into a studio, the kitchen, into a darkroom, while he lived with his wife in a small room at the back.

At the sound of the bell that rang each time the door was opened, Christine rushed to greet the customers, smothering the children with caresses. Decked out in a black smock and an artist's beret, Edouard positioned them before a camera set on a tripod and chanted the familiar air: "Smile for the birdie!" Because customers were few and far between, Christine often had to turn to her father for assistance with the rent and food.

After several months of this Bohemian existence, she gave birth to a son. They called him Pierre. To make Christine's joy perfect, the child—the author—never gave her a moment's peace. The wailing of the nursing infant awoke her in the middle of the night and, in the daytime, followed her right into her work. Possessed of a smattering of psychology, she believed it would be harmful to leave Pierre to cry in vain and, at the slightest sign of colic, pleaded with the doctor to come on the run. As for Edouard, he treated me like a doll, binding my head in scarves and taking endless delight in weighing me and measuring me.

One evening, my parents accepted an invitation to visit Suzanne. The roof of the townhouse was fringed with snow. Scraping his boots on the mat, Edouard said to his wife:

"You'll have to powder your nose, it's red from the cold."

In the vestibule, a maid took their coats and led them down a long hallway with mahogany wainscoting. The air was pungent with the aromas of spices and pipe tobacco. Sounds of laughter drifted through an open doorway, which cast a square of smoky light on the hallway carpet. A fire blazed in the Franklin stove, casting its reflections over the faces of the guests, who reclined on wild animal skins and sofas, guzzling beer. Fluted curtains framed the large double windows, which the ice had rendered opaque.

"We were waiting for you," said Suzanne, who was wearing a tapered black dress covered with silver sequins.

Christine caught sight of herself in a mirror: the rumpled dress, the shiny nose. She realized that her mother-in-law eclipsed her in beauty.

"Where can I freshen up?" she asked.

Suzanne led her into a small room, containing a dressing-table covered with little pots of paint and pomade.

"God, how pregnancy causes a woman to fade!" exclaimed the laundress tactlessly. "You're already losing your shape! You must look after your breasts, my dear. Nursing your little angel will cause them to sag." Then, brandishing a string of pearls, she added: "Would you like these? They're not fake. Everything here is real: the mahogany, the marble, the gold!"

After a final flick of the comb, Christine rose. But the older woman pushed her back into her seat.

"You seem like an intelligent girl, so I'm going to give you a bit of advice. In the future, kill your children in the egg. Then have your husband declared legally incompetent. If not, you'll spend your life cleaning up behind the one and covering up for the other."

"And why not strangle my son and commit my husband to an asylum, while I'm at it? Then poison my father, so I can inherit his wealth without waiting for him to kick off? Oh, I'm not kidding! And now," she added in a tone of disgust, "let's get out of here!"

Back in the living-room, they encountered a pot-bellied colossus chug-a-lugging a steinful of beer, while Edouard clapped out the rhythm with his hands. Without spilling a single drop, the drinker hurled the stein across the room and smashed it against the fire-dogs.

"Bravo, Armand! You're a real man!" exclaimed Suzanne. "Now it's your turn, Edouard!"

Edouard performed the same feat, followed by his brothers, François, a puny fellow who made his living as a pettifogger, Réal, a young man with a moustache and sinister-looking eyes, and Jacques and Paul, blood brothers whose features were distorted from drink and who licked their lips like young wolves over a kill. Dominating this fracas of smashing glasses, which were thrown at random about the room, was Suzanne's exhilarated laughter, as she poured herself glass after glass of champagne. The daughters-in-law had instinctively drawn together in a corner of the room. The fire glowed and crackled, like a big, malevolent, scarlet flower, upon which Armand pissed, while the others sat mutely contemplating the dance of the jet of urine over the walls. Suzanne approached her husband, who sat blissfully smoking his pipe, and pinched his cheek.

"Take a look at my brood!" she declared. "I'm proud of every last one of them! I only wish they were more depraved!"

"All right, old girl, take it easy," Vincent tranquilly replied.

"Oh, I forgot, we must leave the old man in peace to dream of his mistress," she declared, then placing one fist on her hip, she cried: "Armand, let me see your better half!"

The young man docilely pushed a skinny, frightened young woman in front of his mother.

"Have you beaten her yet today?" demanded Suzanne. "Hélène, show us your thighs!"

And she tried to raise the girl's skirt. Then, like some carniverous beast abandoning its prey for yet another, more delectable morsel, she turned her gaze upon Christine, squinting her myopic eyes.

"And here we have the virtuous young heiress, who except for a little luck might have had her baby three months before her marriage!"

Suzanne moistened her lips with the tip of a pale, pointed tongue. Though the woman was generally looked upon as being cynical and grotesque, she was only telling the truth. Did it never occur to people that most human sentiments are artificial and deceitful, that the moment you examine them closely they begin to lose their focus? Every moment of every day, a man entertains unkind thoughts about his partner, thoughts which he keeps to himself, and it is only because of this perpetual dissimulation that love is allowed to survive. Suzanne, on the other hand, laid all her cards on the table, insulting now in order not to have to flatter later on. By deceiving others, one does not run the risk of duping oneself. Cruelty suited this woman well, precluding all possibility of

40

love and pity, things which might lead her astray. She had nine sons, nine times she had given birth, and each time the maternal instinct in her had lost a little more of its ardour. We are a race that craves nourishment and affection; among others, her insensitivity might have been looked upon as being normal.

Suddenly, the wood in the fireplace collapsed in a shower of sparks. Cooled by Suzanne's departure and a little troubled by her parting words, my uncles retired in silence. My father kissed Vincent on the brow and went in search of his coat. He returned to find Christine whispering animatedly with Suzanne:

"And what if Edouard opposes your plan? Or urges you to reconsider?"

"I'll tell him to go to hell. And to take his wife and son with him. Because he's nothing but an accident, the result of a moment's carelessness on my part."

"And do you know what he'd do?" asked Christine arrogantly. "He'd kill you!"

And she gave the older woman a sharp slap, causing her to stagger a little. A thread of blood sprang from the corner of Suzanne's mouth. Sliding her arms into the fur coat that her stupefied husband held for her, my mother dragged Edouard toward the door, ignoring the insults that rained down on her from behind.

The sidewalks were miniature ice-fields. The snowflakes, illuminated and etched in the light of the streetlamps, flew by as if in assault on a fortress. A few rickety old coaches slept beneath their heavy blankets of snow. It seemed to Edouard that the world was slowly winding down, and he thought how nice it would be to stretch out there on the cold ground. Christine walked in step with him, her jet-black hair glowing in the lamplight, her eyes fixed unflinchingly upon her husband's face. Suddenly he turned and, placing his hands beneath her armpits, lifted her from the ground, happy to discover that she was as light as a feather despite her heavy winter clothing.

"My little wife!" he cooed. "My little lovebird!" And he pressed his lips to her brow.

She closed her eyes and murmured, "Promise me you'll never see Suzanne again. If I spoke sharply to her tonight, it was because she asked for it. She's plotting against us."

"You know I can't do that. She's my mother. A part of me belongs to her."

"The worst part. When I saw you getting drunk with your brothers, I found myself scorning you, in spite of myself."

As they were descending a steep slope, she suddenly lost her footing. Edouard reached out to steady her.

"Do you remember those photos we saw of Nagasaki? After that, how can a man believe he isn't building on sand? We have no future, one attitude is as good as another. Who are we to condemn my mother?" He shook his head. "I am the wood from which flutes are made. I have two poles: you and Suzanne."

Christine yielded, but she made it clear that she would not see her mother-in-law again.

"You can use my headaches as an excuse," she said wearily.

He promised to smother her in riches the moment Vincent passed on. The thought of this inheritance obsessed him, nourishing the hatred he felt for the mediocrity of his present condition.

He tried to hide from his family the fact that Christine had broken with them. He bought cakes at a pastry shop, insisting they had come fresh from his wife's oven; he even went so far as to imply that she repented of having slapped Suzanne. The latter insinuated that a good-looking young man like him would be stupid to cling to such an ugly, bad-tempered woman, that a certain high-spirited brunette had exclaimed in disbelief at the news that Edouard was not only married, but faithful to his wife. But my grandmother was wasting her time. Edouard was madly in love with Christine and found the hours away from her interminable.

One evening, the telephone rang. It was my Aunt Hélène.

"Come quick!" she yelled. "They're going to kill your father!"

Edouard was out of the house in a flash. The following morning, a nurse called to inform Christine that her husband was asking for her. She found him in a room resounding with the laughter of the two convalescents. A huge bandage covered his nose, making him look as if he were wearing a helmet. His hazel eyes were bloodshot. In a few disjointed sentences, he explained that he had found Vincent being thrashed by his sons, Armand and Réal, in the living-room.

"The bastards were just playing, they weren't hitting him hard, but *papa* wasn't resisting and his eyes were glazed. As I was about to go to his aid, I saw *maman* standing in a corner of the room, calmly smoking a cigarette. So I let them have their way with me, hoping she would intervene. When my face was a bloody pulp, she yelled, 'Enough!' Then they brought me here."

A few days later, Edouard returned home, the bridge of his nose and both his lips grotesquely swollen. A report in the newspapers stated that, due to failing health, Vincent had decided to turn his company over to a triumvirate made up of his wife and his two sons, Armand and Réal. The rest of his holdings were to be placed in trust for the remaining members of his family. But it's a well-known fact that he who runs after the shoes of a corpse runs the risk of finding himself barefoot.

PART TWO: FLEET-FOOTED TIME

Every man is no more different from other men than he often is from himself—La Rochefoucauld.

PROLOGUE

It rolls through me like a subterranean river. Sometimes I forget its presence, but the moment I stop to listen, I hear it carrying me along with the sound of a thousand torrents. What is it? Thought. I hold my breath and I plunge. A mirror polished smooth by streets and walls, I think, I think . . . There is no rejection in me, I am the sempiternal yes, the antithesis of the void. I am wholly inhabited by the world, to the point of nausea. As full and solid as a hard-boiled egg, I am oblivious to all those viscous, anomalous things that prevail outside the frontiers of my gaze. If I look at a thing long enough, it crystallizes, hardens, seems at a certain moment to emit only one colour and one sound. But I know that this is a deliberate deception, and it is from this duplicity that I derive my reverence for chaos. A fable, a hoax, a pipe-dream dispersed by the wind, I ingest all the impostures, all the adulterations. I could never outlive truth, a core of silence in the midst of all the swarming, creeping, capering atoms. O Death, you who derive your existence through me, I long for you, you supreme, indispensible lie!

In order to give birth to the word—and to myself, with it— I must be shifty, evasive. *Little, big, high, low.* Like a frog, I emerge from the depth to give breath to the qualifiers, the nouns. Does this mean, then, that the trees, the stars, the rivers are mute? Or do they together unleash a cry whose echo is never-ending? In that long sentence that has meaning only for the illiterate, is man the comma or the key phrase?

I shall flow through those domains reverberating with past and future voices and draw your so-called phantoms up into

44

the light of day. Nothing is unreal, I tell you. Reproduced to infinity, your dreams encounter that implausible being who spends his time tirelessly imagining you. Scrabbling to and fro, like crabs stranded on the last beach in the universe, where the void is dashed to pieces against the jetties of stars! On the terrace of this monastery, I interrogate the moon, a gold button in a navy-blue vest. But I have already divined its reply, which is the same as that of the cowering crags and the glutinous pools. "Present!' they all cry in unison, rearing up on the crest of time, like blind, obstinate idols. Yes, they are always present, in all places, at all times, prevailing in the face of the centuries that toss them about like pebbles in a wave. I sense their presence, illuminated by the rising sun, repeating their rallying cry. Despite its paltry appearance, the smallest pebble has the power to crush us, for it fills all eternity. We, the malingerers, the deserters, the never-there, puncture and riddle our past with incendiary bullets. But that blackguard is not easily subdued, and our all-out war against him is doomed in advance to defeat. Mummies wrapped in yet more and more bandages, we strike a pose and smile, hoping to leave a favourable impression. *Look at the birdie!* The birdie pops out and swallows us like a fly.

The black branches of the skeletal trees make chinks in the distant sky. The fog winds about the trunks of the trees like a big grey caterpillar. That long, white depression in the earth must be the river. The monks scurry about the brioche of their monastery, like distracted insects exposed to the light of day. I've taken refuge here to purge myself, to probe my entrails, to remove my heart and lay it on a white handkerchief that will soak up all the blood. Meanwhile, I light the fire in the crematory oven of memories and sentiments.

A quarter-century ago, by a stroke of unprecedented ill luck, we came into being. In the void in which we frolicked like atoms, innocuously coming together and separating again, some irresponsible creature saw fit to introduce his seed. Then, like a cancer, we began to suppurate and grow. A final sweep

45

of the periscope, and we emerged. All hands on deck! Every moment of every day, thousands of these little bubbles break on the surface of the world. It is called birth.

A white light was trained on the stage and the actors leapt from the wings: a truculent father in baggy pants with accordion pleats, a mother with the smell of the sea in her hair. All I had to do was retrace my steps to bring the play to a halt, to send it winding back to its beginnings. But, somewhere between the dawn and the night, I caught a glimpse of the bird-smiles of men and I left the darkness behind me to sail toward the light. I became one of you.

Syringes filled with a deadly poison will glitter on the counter of the tea-room. I shall exact the price of death of my trembling fingers. Urine and blood, the lips contorted in pain: must one love all this to be a man? The triumphant henchmen, the victims who kill: must one be proud of being a man?

I shall inject the substance into the small of my left arm. . . . So short a time it takes me to die that already my footprints are effaced from the earth, already the shadows are settling about me. . . . But nothing around me will have changed, my heart will continue to beat. I won't know whether I am dead or alive. Perhaps I shall already be part of the earth, the flowers and the fire.

A woman will say to me:

"You see that river? It's called the Lude. To find what you're seeking, you must drink of its waters."

I shall set out, filled with hope. I shall visit strange cities and skies in which night will vanish in a swarming of giant stars, and always on the horizon the Lude will unfold the turquoise lace of its waters, which will be lost in time as others are lost in the sea.

And it may happen that I shall live, vulnerable to love and hatred. But I shall have only one future. I shall be neither the conqueror nor the reeling drunkard. I shall never overflow my banks, like a river in flood, filling up the roads and ditches of the countryside.

That we dream of so many mad things does not surprise me;
what surprises me is that we believe ourselves to be the ones
who do and think all these things—Lichtenberg.

EMERGING FROM CHAOS

What is that river flowing at the bottom of my memory, as
distant as a dream that takes flight at the moment of awakening? A clear, sparkling rent in the curtain of spruce and birch,
the sandy river, with logs strewn across its surface, jostled by
the eddies and foam. Near the shore, more tranquil water, with
patches of light and shadow beneath the low-hanging branches
of oak trees, and a wooden dock whose planks are covered
with a cold, slimy moss. Frothy water, breaking into a thousand layers of crystalline lacework at the foot of the dam,
constructed many years ago by Guillaume. And the powerful
odour of resin floating in the air, like the aromas of childhood,
pervading the underbrush with its carpet of brown pine
needles that crackle underfoot. And the shafts of light that
descend from the treetops. And the blueberries culled from
along the bone-white roadside. . . . All these things lie buried
within me, like the seeds of future harvests.

I was four years old. Already, Father, your ambitions had
been shattered into a thousand small sharp fragments. You
were walking with Guillaume, seemingly attentive to his
words, but your gaze wandered over the Laurentian Hills,
which you told me had been carved by glaciers millions of
years ago. You laughed when I ran toward you, the black
spaniel at my heels. You took me in your arms and tickled my
face with your moustache. At times I was afraid of you, like
the day you shot the bluebird caught in the skunk trap. It was
flapping its wings and making a frightful noise; then there
was a burst of thunder from your gun and a trail of blood on
the dark earth. At dusk, you told me the story of a lamb caught
in a thicket that I freed and tamed.

How can I tell you that the most human, most painful part

47

of all this for me derived from those naïve stories you told me during our occasional canoe outings? You believed that this life was only a transitory thing, that it was necessary to sacrifice yourself to others. You forgave me for calling your convictions into doubt. Now that these pages have carried me up to the age of recollection, to the point at which I can speak directly of you, I should like to be able to bring that great song of yours rising out of the depths of the audible, out of the long roads of silence.

We spent our summers at Guillaume's country home, a large brown house that sat in the middle of an emerald lawn. I remember a grey, uncertain dawn, when the leaves fluttered in the muggy wind like a thousand small fingers gloved in silk and the feathers of the crows were still misted with night. I shivered, making what was perhaps my first discovery of evil, its terrible beauty. Suddenly, the stones and the flowers in the garden were drained of all light. All of nature began to crackle, attacked by an invisible flame. It was raining. On the verandah, the scraping of a chair moved by my grandfather sounded painfully strange to my ears. During my nap, a black wasp circled for a long time above my cot, the quick beating of its wings creating a shadowy corolla about its body, which, etched against the white background of the ceiling, resembled a star in the night sky as seen in a negative. In the midst of my disgust, did I sense perhaps that I was contemplating my own death?

It will take place in winter, following an evening of debauchery. A little drunk, I shall step into a phone booth to call a taxi. When I give the name of the street, the voice at the other end of the line will snigger, insisting that this street does not exist. Then I shall follow an old man in a black overcoat into a cold house.

"You have been dead such a long time, *papa*," I shall say to the stranger, "why do you come back now?"

He will shake his head, while affixing a stamp to an air-mail letter.

"Go and mail this for me," he will say.

And suddenly I will understand: no street, no house, nothing. . . . Before I die, Edouard will smile at me one last time.

One Sunday, I was taken into an abandoned chapel that my family had decided to restore. There was a smell of mildew and wet earth. The trees scratched at the windows, my footsteps echoed hollowly on the uneven floor. Before me was a white, rectangular box with a cross over it. I was told that I was in the House of God. I didn't want to leave.

In my bedroom, an immense space surrounded by shadows, a night-light in the shape of a sleeping child's head loomed out of the darkness. A mosaic of light and darkness, from which there emanated at times the thin sounds of a music-box. Black streets intersected by alleys, Swiss cheese moon above the rooftops. Birthdays, faintly coloured by tiny candles stuck into the icing of a cake.

Happiness. Christine, in her tailor-made suit, her hair dishevelled, runs before me. She has taken me to see the grey, dusty block of her old school. Now, she laughs as we climb aboard the ferry. Wind, gulls, children. On all sides, whistles and cries. The mooring-ropes are cast off. Leaning on the rails, I watch Lévis recede, its tiny houses scattered over the cliff-tops like sweets in a confectioner's window. To my left, where the river widens, squats a red bridge, arched like a rainbow. When we reach the farther shore, we do not disembark but stand waving to children diving from the wharf into the black, oily water. Proud of his gold stripes, the captain smiles at us. A young man with a big green tie says something that causes my mother to blush. But what do I care? The boat departs again. *"A Saint-Malo, beau port de mer, trois beaux navires sont arrivés,"* sings Christine. And this song, to my ears, is like a promise of paradise, where the arches resemble those of the bridge that drops into the water at the point where sky and water meet. Back from our excursion, we move down the street, the long line of telephone poles standing crookedly and haphazardly against the flaming wall of the horizon, the houses looking as if they had been blacked-out for centuries, in a silence that is more profound than a simple absence of sound; and all these things impress themselves upon me with a tranquillizing urgency. The world is just as it should be, I give it my assent.

Ginette, the daughter of one of Edouard's brothers, was for me the incarnation of a captive princess. Draped in a sheet that fell about my feet in a thousand folds, I did battle with the monsters born of my cousin's fear. To compel her admiration, I ventured into the attic and returned from that bogeyman's den with an old-fashioned dress, in which I attired the young damsel. I longed for her to nibble my neck, to take me in her arms following a simulated battle. The similarity of our physiognomies was a source of endless amusement for the adults: Ginette's long hair and bright grey skirt made her my feminine double, whom I took pleasure in aping. While her father, the prototype of the tyrant, strode about the dining-room, Ginette showed me the marks left by the blows he had dealt her. My powerlessness to shield her from evil left me speechless with rage. When my Uncle Armand summoned her to follow him, she kissed me furtively, the shadow of a reproach in her eyes.

The truce between my father and his family came to an end. Weeks, months passed, with no news from Ginette. As the result of a few indiscreet inquiries, I learned that Armand beat his wife regularly, and my fears for my cousin emboldened me to demand that I be taken to see her. Christine took a switch to me. Crouched in a corner, I pleaded for mercy. Over the years, my cousin's features grew blurred in my mind, leaving only a glowing memory, with which I knew I would one day have to confront reality.

Johanne, a young girl with the slender beauty of a sunflower, who liked to play Cowboys and Indians. Daniel, with the grey pallor and drawn features of a sickly child. Alain, the youngest son of a poor family, whose father went into debt collecting art books. And Jean, a taciturn adolescent who practised archery, fished for tadpoles and taught my sister to skate. At the end of the street, behind a thick palisade of maple trees, stood a great mansion, whose deceased owner was reputed to haunt the labyrinth of hallways that might have been designed by a mad architect. It was said that a treasure in gems was hidden behind those walls. I tried once to visit the place, but an old man barred my way; I could have sworn he had a rifle in his hand. A few days later, Alain told us:

"The old Englishman's treasure is mine!"

But since he refused to show it to us and continued to go about in rags and to smell of urine, no-one believed him.

One morning, as I was leaving for school, several policemen emerged from the neighbour's house, carrying a stretcher covered with a sheet. I saw my sister standing apart from the crowd that had gathered about the ambulance and the police van, a dazed look on her face. That evening, I learned that Jean-the-taciturn had butchered our neighbours with an axe and that my sister had discovered their bodies in the bloodsplattered living-room. People hypocritically expressed pity for the assassin's father and offered him assistance, but he remained shut up in his house, emerging only at night.

These acts of violence were quickly forgotten, thanks to an article in the newspaper which told of a number of victims of accidents who, at the moment of death, had seen a red, driverless van graze past them then vanish into the fog. In the evening, whenever I heard the screech of tires on the pavement, I sensed the presence behind me of the mysterious vehicle, whose mad, indifferent race through the city was an indication of how the world would one day manage without me. Not a messenger from another world, but one from this world in a state of transformation.

The ambulance has halted on the seashore. Two male nurses are dragging a little man from the water. He is trembling violently, his face is turning purple. Unaware of the danger involved, he plucked a jellyfish from the waves, watching as it stroked him lazily with its poisonous tentacles. Now, the little man will die.

We had engaged a country girl by the name of Fleurette as a nursemaid. Pretty, buxom and bright, she had always treated me kindly. One morning, I found her room empty, the bed still made. I awakened Christine at the very moment the poor girl was trying to re-enter the house unnoticed, her black suit all rumpled. My mother dismissed her on the spot. Before leaving, Fleurette gazed at me for a moment, then, setting down her two suitcases, kissed me on the forehead. A sickly sweet odour emanated from her. Christine seized my arm and pulled me violently away. My nose pressed to the living-room window, I watched my nursemaid return in the early hours of the morning to her home in the country. There, her adventures with the local boys eventually drove her mother to suicide. With the aid of a long pole, Fleurette fished the body from the pond, where she had found it floating face-down. This scene was recounted to me by my parents, as an example of the disastrous results of sin.

Because the toilet had backed up and flooded the bathroom, I was obliged to pee in a tin can. I had been shut up in the dining-room. The lack of curtains on the French doors threatened me with exposure. The metal walls of the can felt cold and rough against my thighs. Reduced to the most elemental aspect of my biological self, I was mortified by that ineluctable equation of my body (which I would gladly have willed into non-existence) and base matter. It is the sirens one desires: their lower halves are bestial. By dint of setting the spirit and the flesh in constant opposition to each other, I had come to see the two as irreconcilable. Because I had denied the real world, it gave me such a drubbing that I was then obliged to defy God. My disbelief must stem from some mystical crisis.

We were taught hatred, but I learned only fear. The nuns gave us comic strips that told of an eventual Communist takeover in Canada. Once the Prime Minister had been assassinated, men in mustard-coloured uniforms with red stars on their caps tortured the priests and gunned down the devout, who prayed in secret to the Virgin.

School. A building flanked by two towers. Interminable corridors filled with marching, pink-cheeked urchins. Shouts, impatient flittings to and fro, the pungent odours of a menagerie. My classroom: thick glass windows, opening slantwise at the top, drenching us with the light from a sky that hung captive in the narrow space between the church and the gymnasium. It was in this azure strip, sometimes resembling a washed-out plank, sometimes looking very distant, when clouds passed over it or it was filled with stars—it was there that I read the seasons and the hours.

I lived in the suburbs of Quebec City. I took the streetcar each morning to school. How proud I was the day the conductor refused me entry, seeing me standing on the sidewalk with an empty beer bottle! Aside from my schoolmates, chubby urchins with short-cropped hair, the tram carried students to the public schools, young ruffians who poked fun at our neat appearance. The filthy streets were filled with pale-faced businessmen and silent immigrants in thin black overcoats, all hurrying somewhere or other. A friend explained the workings of rockets to me, while the long pole squeaked along the overhead wire. Vague, fleeting forms slid past on either side, moving toward some hypothetical abyss behind my head. The images of a life that shook and trembled without ever going off the tracks, a convulsion of pathetic scenes that offered little risk to our safety, no ditch in which order might momentarily be reversed, the wheels pointed toward the sky and spinning aimlessly.

Outside Boston, the Charles River flows nonchalantly between two sandy shores. The forest, humming with mosquitoes, is drenched with a soft, creamy light. Through the foliage can be discerned the squat mass of the abbey, which has been my home for the past few weeks. Father Freeman, a tranquil colossus, takes in the tremulous setting with a wide, sweeping gesture and drawls:

"Such beauty! Such order! How can one fail to see God's

handiwork in it?"

He smiles, revealing a mouthful of crooked, yellow teeth. Their faces hidden by their cowls, the monks move toward the refectory. All this may be no more than a web spun by God.

Wouldn't it be enough, in the end, if one wished to set one's life in order, to learn to pay atention? The scrupulous attention of the rope-walker as he moves slowly along his wire? The important thing is not to fall, for there is no net, no second chance to reach the farther side. The very slow, very beautiful fall of a comet toward the sun; the drop in a roller-coaster, paradoxically like the abrupt flight of one's entire being; the descent into Orpheus' underworld—nothing comparable here to the plunge of Lucifer or an unfortunate trapeze artist, who see themselves approaching their end through the sudden appearance beneath them of the void, an impression Christ himself must have experienced during his ordeal in the desert, dazzling cities laid out at his feet, all his to possess if only he would worship Satan—in other words, hurl himself into the gulf.

THE SELLER OF STARS

For a long while, Edouard held onto his photographic studio only by the skin of his teeth. But, little by little, his few remaining customers deserted him, while the rent continued to go up. He lost a great deal of money and, without Guillaume's assitance, eventually had to declare bankruptcy. He was then obliged to seek other employment. Confident of his "talent for business," he bought twenty, fifteen-foot, sheet-iron stars, each equipped with red, blue and yellow neon tubes that clicked on and off at regular intervals. Their patent bad taste and gaudiness promised to bring customers flocking to the most modest french-fry stand, not to mention the shoemaker's, the manufacturer's, the priest's—to all of whom Edouard, carried away by a sudden flair for salesmanship, hoped to sell these objects in pairs: one for the front of the business in the guise of a sign, the other to adorn the roof. The first morning, he rubbed his hands together, as if to say: "Today, Quebec! Tomorrow, the world!" He gathered the family together to view the metallic monster he had set up in the living-room, laughing as we leapt back in terror, blinded by the fireworks display. After we had sweated and strained to lift the star onto the trailer behind his car, a look of alarm came over his face: how on earth was he going to lug that horror about all alone? But he shrugged, lit a cigar and took off in a cloud of dust, singing a bel canto air at the top of his lungs. With his jet-black hair and his elegant moustache, he might have passed for an immigrant who had just stepped off the boat from Naples.

He returned that evening, muttering invectives against the incomparable stupidity of the middle class, which was incapable of grasping the benefits to be derived from this marvellous new form of publicity. Christine filled the bath with hot, salty water, in which our hero soaked his aching back. Then he ate a hearty meal, demonstrating with bold gestures and half-censored blasphemies how he had sung the praises of his product to an insolent, skeptical Jew. He improvised, while the little mother egged him on with sarcastic remarks and the children doubled up with laughter. Reassured and comforted by our encouragement, he scoured the want ads, convinced that he would find there the road leading to the land of milk and honey. A few weeks later, selling off the remainder of his stars at cutthroat prices, he embarked upon a new campaign: peddling orange juice to those members of society who were drugged, deadened and disabled by alcohol, coffee and tobacco. Armed with a pamphlet on vegetarianism and a quart of yellowish liquid, he swooped down upon restaurants and taverns, burning to convert the entire city to his "orangist ideas," as my mother jokingly called them. But he was preaching in the desert and, despite all his efforts, did not succeed in making a living. Guillaume still had to help him make ends meet.

There was nothing less communal than our home life. Each member of the family holed up in his room, avoiding contact with the others even when emerging to go to the toilet. My parents abhorred all noise; I held my breath each time I made a move. Fortunately, I enjoyed reading. Meanwhile, my sister sat in her room and counted the fly specks on the milky globe in the ceiling. Only meals interfered with our mutual isolation. As regular as a piece of sheet music, they were the occasion of quarrels and scenes, always the same ones.

The kitchen window, which looked out on the backyard, was kept covered with a muslin curtain. (One day when I raised it, Edouard, who was just then coming into the room, grew pale: "Close that curtain! You'll have the neighbours spying on us!") Ensconced at one end of the speckled, salmon-coloured table, my father would sniff the food, ever alert for an opportunity to exert his authority. Had Christine failed to freshen her makeup? Since she invariably either humoured him or remained resolutely silent, he would then turn to me: "Don't put your elbows on the table! Don't slurp your soup!" He would glare at me pugnaciously and, if I scowled, he would explode: "Look at that child! You'd think he was displeased with me!" With time, I learned to adopt Christine's attitude, submitting silently to the slightest rebuke. That left Solange, a little blond girl with a turned-up nose and a low, stubborn brow. Far from yielding like the rest of us, she would provoke my father and argue with him, showing no fear whatever for Edouard's blows, which were admittedly rather light.

She knew all the chinks in his armour. "When a person is unemployed ... Is it true our grandparents are rich?" One evening, following a particularly malevolent insult, he yelled: "That girl is the spitting image of my mother!" This notion quickly took root in his mind, becoming an obsession. He would discourse endlessly upon the subject of heredity, little realizing that through these digs he was obliging my sister to

56

play the role of the evil Suzanne. A sempiternal wet blanket, he took violent opposition to our laughter, on the grounds that it was ill-mannered. Moulded in the image of his perpetual sullenness, we slouched about, parading our prudishness and our melancholy for all to see.

But when Christine judged that one of my father's whims had gone too far, he was quick to plead for forgiveness. If she left him alone with us, he would badger us with questions: "When did your mother say she'd be back? Did she look upset when she left?" Since he was unable to tolerate silence, he would harp upon his disappointments, bemoaning the fate that had cast in his lot with a people as worthless of consideration as the French Canadians. No-one found favour in his eyes. The English? A race of grocers, who had behaved abominably toward Napoleon, the most noble of heroes. The French? Hypocrites and smooth-talkers, every last one of them. The Jews, above all, met with his disapproval, for their practice of ruining honest businesses. Ensconced in his armchair, he would find fault with the entire universe, falling silent at the slightest sound that might signal Christine's return. The longer she remained away, the gloomier he became. The atmosphere was dark and heavy, rain lashed the windows of the living-room. We might be famished, but he would have let us starve rather than lift a hand to feed us, which he saw as a woman's task. At the table, wasn't it the worst sin against etiquette to anticipate Christine's move and to serve yourself? He harboured all those supremely impractical notions cherished by so many great men and dreamers, at times resembling the knight with the sad countenance himself.

As a child, he and his friends had often re-enacted the Battle of the Plains of Abraham, and standing now before the cannons that still squatted menacingly above the river, his only explanation for our defeat was to attribute it to divine malediction. Didn't the historians themselves state that Walker's fleet had foundered because of our prayers and that the conquest had been a punishment for our sins?

In the name of a vague universalism, he disowned his own people. "It was nationalism that decimated Europe," he said again and again. He railed against our dialect and our customs, seeing them as the traits of a second-class people. Far better to be a turncoat, to "become" English, than to stagnate amongst that pious riff-raff. He took pleasure in laying claim to a Scottish ancestor, as if this somehow set him apart from his fellows. The rudiments of the English language, which he had picked up in the Army, he displayed with pride, pleased to discover that we understood none of it. On the other hand, he would not tolerate strangers poking fun at us, and had even been known to strike someone for a harmless allusion.

I have depicted Edouard as a perennial grouch, but on rare occasions his gloominess and meanness mysteriously vanished. I recall picnics on the banks of swift-running streams, when he would dance and climb into the trees, yelling like a savage. (Didn't you once confess to me, Father, that you still felt as young as a man in his twenties? And, today, at times, gazing at the way the light plays games with the shape of a house or a cloud, I wonder which half of you was the false one: the dark or the light?)

THE WATCH KEY

Already effaced from my mind by his repeated absences and his unmistakably weak character, Edouard was further eclipsed during the dinners to which Guillaume invited me. On the other hand, the latter told me a number of touching stories, like the one of the beggar who had been turned away one Christmas from all the houses in a hamlet, except that of a poor man, who, at dawn, discovered his cellar full of food and gold. As for the vagabond, he had vanished without a trace, not even leaving any footprints in the snow.

My grandfather had a great veneration for manual labour,

and I blushed at my awkwardness whenever he tore the hammer or shovel from my hands to tidy up some job I had botched. One day, while accompanying him on a visit to the home of one of his servants, I took one look at the run-down flat and exclaimed, "How ugly!" I can still feel the imprint of his palm on my cheek. He moved with ease amongst people of all classes and, once, at the beach, even shared the meal of a fat Jewess whom he had met only a half-hour before. One evening, when he was explaining the reasons for his success, my sister retorted, with a malice rendered keen by the sarcastic rejoinders with which she normally met my father's insults: "You're bragging a little, aren't you?"

"Hold your tongue, you little idiot!" he exclaimed, tearing his napkin in his rage. Never again did I hear him speak of his youth in our presence.

My grandfather's face was so emaciated you could actually see the bonework of the skull. The incongruity of that warm, virile voice emanating from a body that had long been deprived of all grace, was at once comic and awesome. I recall him standing one day before the window, his back stooped, gazing at the snow that the wind was piling about the house. Rubbing his hands together, as if the glacial vastness of all the outdoors had sent a shiver through his bones, he said:

"Dying is nothing. When a piece of meat rots, it's only right you should throw it away. What scares me is paralysis, a blood clot on the brain. When that happens to a man, he becomes a living corpse. Surviving, they call it, but that's the only time death has any meaning, because then you're conscious of it."

He was chewing a piece of gum, its minty odour perfuming the air about him.

"If that happened to me, I'd come to hate myself, for not being able to escape such a fate."

I was afraid to say anything, and he returned to his look-out at the window. For a long while, all I could hear were the sounds of his chewing.

One foot in the grave, Guillaume became a walking drugstore. At night, he often suffered from chest pains, awakening in the belief that his heart had stopped beating. He would grope for his pills on the bedside table. Alone in the darkness. The silence stretching all about him. Death slowly building its nest in his body. Then his fingertips would register a faint beating, and his boat would raise anchor and move on. Though hale and hearty, he was not one to exert himself. So that, gradually, through atrophy, his limbs and vital organs began to seize up, while his bloated belly hung like a heavy sack between his thighs. Each morning, the hairs on the pillow and the tangles in the hairbrush were carefully counted and inspected. His eyesight began to fail him: he acquired thick glasses. And still he hung on, dispensing reluctantly with his nine lives, forcing himself each day to walk a little farther about the house than he had done the day before.

The worst part of it was that you were alone. Your entire family consisted of a wife, who was deaf, and a daughter who had married the first man who came along. A life, when it's over, is something you can hold in the palm of your hand and toss over your shoulder. A life, when it's behind you, has about as much substance as candy floss. You flatter yourself that you're serving your fellow man, but that's simply a way of excusing your own selfish ambitions. Of course, you'd written a couple of stageplays, which you reread now on the sly, but you knew the moment you were in the ground your wife would burn all those impious texts.

"Mindless, pretentious creatures," you had once called the lovers, the poets, the dreamers. Your dreams had been realized with concrete and steel. Now, you contemplated the world you had built and subsequently betrayed, repeating in consternation: "That isn't so, no, that isn't it at all." You couldn't listen to the simplest song, the simplest soap opera, without breaking into tears. Because of an unfortunate predilection, you had placed reason above all else; and now, when you invoked it in the face of the gulf—which was not at all "eternal" and "fathomless": after all, a grave is only six feet deep—it left you in the lurch. So you submitted, comforting yourself with your Yuban coffee, your Kleenex-tissues-as-soft-as-down and your Player's-the-man's cigarette.

Then one day—as the result of some stupidity that you swallowed whole and gagged on—you decided to take yourself in hand. Memories of your youth evoked sunshine in the dead of winter, sand the colour of snow, fine, warm sand. You invited your daughter and your son-in-law to take a trip with you to California.

Before his departure for Los Angeles, I went to bid Guillaume farewell. I found him studying a map, on which a red line had been pencilled to indicate his itinerary. Madeleine was stuffing a suitcase to overflowing. He refused the hand I offered him. Giving me an ironical look, he said:

"Forget the formalities. Why should you come to say good-bye? Sentiments are for women and old men like me."

Reproaching myself for my display of emotion, I turned and left without a word.

The initial stages of the journey were uneventful, characterized by the monotony of unfamiliar cities as seen through the windows of a car. But during the fifth night of the trip, in a roadside motel, Madeleine awoke to discover her husband suffering heart pains. His bulging eyes rolled about in his skull and faint blue circles spread outward from his gaping lips, like ripples in a pool into which a stone has been cast. Despite the serum administered by a doctor from the neighbouring village, he lost the use of his limbs. Christine tried to calm her mother, while Edouard fretted and fumed. It is said that, following the death of Tamerlain, his generals transported him to Samarkand without daring to part the curtains of the litter in which the body lay slowly decomposing. A similar fear prevented my parents from washing my grandfather or changing his sheets. Finally, Madeleine got a grip on herself and took charge of the invalid, just as she had once done with Guillaume's mother. Soon the room reeked of ammonia, and the dying man, gleaming like a piece of porcelain, his arms crossed soberly over his chest, lost his forbidding air. His glassy eyes no longer looked so strange, and conversations were conducted in normal voices, despite his presence in the room.

"I'll move in with you, if you like, *maman*," said Christine. "It'll take both of us to look after him."

But the older woman demurred, already a little jealous of her patient.

After a few weeks, Guillaume's condition began to improve. He was able to move his arms and legs a little and utter a few words. His mind was still intact. My parents, bored to death in that little village in the heart of the Arizona desert, took the car and explored a little farther each day. One morning, leaving Guillaume in Madeleine's care, they departed in the direction of the Rio Grande.

Guillaume and I had often taken walks together in the dirty streets of the city, through which a moist autumn wind had prowled. With his retirement, my companion had stowed his top hat in the attic and returned to wearing his work cap and jacket wherever he went. However much thoughts of his approaching end may have tormented him, he feigned an indifference to the subject. A long, worm-shaped cloud stretched toward Ile d'Orléans. The sight of my grandfather's thin, bony hands and stubby fingernails reminded me of the time he had held a pansy to my nose, its brown and yellow velvet petals quivering in the moist air. Suddenly, we were surrounded by shouting children: "Ugly old bum, fall on your bum!" And, in his old rags, my grandfather did look a bit shabby. But he was baffled by those jeers, and while I chased off the urchins, who dispersed in a cloud of laughter, he swallowed one of the capsules that whipped his heart into a frenzy and that he bitterly called his "watch key." Following a life sacrificed to the pursuit of wealth, he appeared as destitute and powerless as he had in his adolescence, when he had been mocked by the same rich kids. It was as if some philosopher- god had decided to enlighten him as to the vanity of ambition. With his encounter with those children, the circle had closed for Guillaume, every bit as cruelly as it had for Oedipus when he learned the secret of his birth.

Did he have that scene in mind, I wonder, when, taking advantage of Madeleine's nap, he left his air-conditioned room in the motel? He was not acting on impulse, because for several days he had concealed the fact that he could actually walk. Behind the motel lay the desert, crushed beneath a flaming sky. Thick-limbed cacti stood in stark profile against the bald, mauve mountains. Here absolute silence reigned, as if the vast space had been walled in, accentuating the strangeness of the needle-like peaks and yawning chasms that stretched into the distance, like the ruins of some ancient civilization. Guillaume made his way slowly through the undergrowth. The sun, which hung for a moment on the horizon, suddenly dropped from the sky. A final gush of light and it was night. The plain began to vibrate with the singing of crickets, lurking in the craggy folds of the earth; they seemed to be saying that life is good, that death is nothing, that millions of stars are born every moment.

The next morning, Edouard found my grandfather's body a short distance from the road. Beside it lay the "watch key" capsules, each one carefully crushed. The white powder that trickled from them had kept Guillaume alive for years. His body was returned by refrigerator car to Quebec, where it was buried in St. Charles Cemetery.

I threw the rat into the little hole in the ground. The corpse had already turned black. It had a rank odour and crumbled like a lump of dry mud when it hit the earth. Nearby, a dragonfly, its steel-blue colour and erratic flight sending a shiver down my spine, flitted over the surface of the pond, which, with its pockets of frogs' eggs and its stagnant black waters, resembled a witch's brew. I liked to kill birds, especially in the autumn, when they stood out clearly against the sky on the leafless branches. I left their soft little bodies lying in the mud, so as to observe their decomposition at close range, until the winter snows came and covered them up.

I had taken a job with a charitable organization. All day long, I transported boxes full of religious tracts on a small handcart. In a dusty basement, beneath the gaze of a Sacred Heart image, I erected pyramids and laid out walls of paper. A priest had covered the concrete walls with pious sayings.

Do not blaspheme, for God can hear you, went one of these, painted in green letters against a grey background.

My day began before sunrise with a cup of coffee drunk on the run in the company of several truckers, then I buried myself in those catacombs, which lent my complexion the aura of old parchment and did permanent damage to my lungs, emerging only when the neon lights of the neighbourhood bars flicked on. At noon, every day, a secretary entertained me with accounts of her successive abortions, inveighing against all males, while I sat silently munching my hamburger and french fries. Solitude has always played havoc with my digestion, prompting me to entertain thoughts that are not particularly cheerful.

After work, I wrapped myself up warmly and moved in the direction of the bus-stop, near which a one-armed man stood cranking his barrel-organ. At the top of a skyscraper, a spotlight pivoted absurdly about, as if it couldn't make up its mind what design to trace with its long, luminous fingers. Stamping my feet, I watched the corner for the appearance of the squat, red-and-white vehicle, which would be crammed with homebound workers, all coughing down one another's necks. The blast of a car horn caused me to jump. Was it a friend, stopping to give me a lift? I saw myself suddenly in the eyes of that driver: a shivering, bleary-eyed ruffian. All trace of my real self had suddenly vanished, only my reflection remained. All the subterfuges and the chimeras that allowed me to exist had mysteriously disappeared. As stupefied as a soldier torn apart by an exploding shell, I peered at the driver of the car, outside of whose gaze I seemed to have no existence. The one we see in the mirror, the one whose hunger, habits and recollections eternally hound us, is both our guard and our prisoner: only his destruction will liberate us. While happiness is the product of a mawkish illusion and unhappiness, of an excess of complacency, lucidity is born of an indifference like the one I felt at that moment. But rarely are we given the opportunity to come face to face with ourselves in that way; and when we do, it is always when we least expect it. God alone can keep his own company with impunity. Our ultimate rendezvous with ourselves is set for the day of our death.

The traffic light turned green, the cars began to move, and I realized suddenly that there had been a mistake, that no-one had stopped for me. I fretted at the slowness of the bus. Brandishing his stump, the cripple continued to play his little tune to the accompaniment of the whistling wind.

Scouring the labyrinth of my memories, I continually run up against the same sense of futility that confronts me today. Held fast by my anxieties before a moment of time that it would be vain to call the present, I scrutinize my past and see in it almost as many shadows and abysses as I do in the future. Satiated with the world, I find myself dispossessed of myself —and if I write *I*, it is at least partly in a spirit of derision. But I continue to entertain the hope of illuminating the darkness and regulating the chaos, of finding myself at the end of this narrative with something more than a number of darkened pages. Art—mine, in the instance—should possess the power, by means of various somersaults and pirouettes, to shed light upon the *me* that has not yet come into being. So I shall paint myself without artifice and without restraint. I know, of course, that death is only brought nearer by the attempt to mute the colours and to throw down the stones; but, without actually taking up the challenge, I shall persist obstinately in my quest. Of all the tunnels I excavate, perhaps one will lead me from the hubbub of the exterior world into the definitive silence of truth.

If it is conceded that the portrait the writer paints of himself can never coincide with the real self, the act of writing (unless one depicts oneself as a writer) being an act of transformation, it is obvious that my ambition is as absurd as trying to find the philosopher's stone. The spaces between words, no longer than the span of an insect's life, represent a time that is forever irretrievable. But here, as in a distorting mirror, there is no straight line, no form that does not alter with the slightest movement of the viewer. It is said that, during the gladiatorial contests, Nero rested his eyes by observing the action through a concave emerald. I must not succumb to the temptation to seek relief from reality, to reduce literature to the level of fastidiousness.

The wind came up, the storm broke. I leaned against the railing. With the sound of many goatskins exploding, the rain lashed the wall of the monastery at the point where it joined the wing of the church. That corner, with its patch of glaucous grass, its heap of crumbled stones glittering like gems, its bare earth pitted with cavities of bubbling mud; those rough, scaly boards, the colour of dead leaves; that salubrious air over which hung a mouse-grey sky; and myself, my hands plunged in my pockets, shivering on that spray-swept verandah. Much more deliquescent than the rain, the wall I was contemplating penetrated me to the very marrow of my bones, becoming for a moment another wall, one I had watched years before beneath a similar downpour, the wall of Guillaume's villa. And I knew that, in the nearby fir grove, crows were diving into the undergrowth, which was rank with the odour of wet earth and charged with electrified air; and that, when I went back indoors to get warm, I would find my father reciting passages from the Bible and Christine stammering in terror, her legs tucked tightly beneath her. It was all as clear to me as the mauve ruts that streaked the sandy road and the bloated waters of the Cartier River that had been transformed by the backwash into a torrent of seething bubbles. My childhood unfolded there on the abbey wall like some phantasmagoria. I sensed that I was very much alone, an object collapsing in on itself.

I raised my eyes to the sky, scored wth wine-coloured veins and criss-crossed with laces of pure light. In the sober cities, I had forgotten that each word resounds in a silence that stretches all the way to Venus, that we are children of the Earth, a wandering planet that is no more than an ocellus in the spreading tail of the universe. In the dark night separating the galaxies, floats the pollen of worlds we shall never know. And, on one of these, my brown, streaming wall may one day be re-erected. Perhaps, in the void, God hears the same door closing on itself into infinity. Just as these words that I weave have been murmured by a thousand other mouths before me. We shall not perish, we shall return; and, with us, the dawns with their enchanting trees and flowers, and this coffee I am drinking, and this scratched desk, and this metal ashtray....

The monks were praying, their faces hidden in their rough cowls. Many champions had died for that cross that was nailed to the refectory wall. Robins were warbling in the garden; through the window, I watched them hop about like fretful little businessmen, one wing folded as if to clasp a briefcase. With a slight toss of their branches, the elms bade farewell to the dark clouds that jostled one another on the horizon. When grace was said, the monks took their seats at the long table, imploring me to follow suit.

Like a fussy housekeeper, Spring scoured the sky and hung the branches of the trees with green bonbons. For what *pièce de boulevard* were these roses replanted and these lawns re-painted each year? Spring, for me, is the sound of my heels striking the cement sidewalk and the snow melting in the gutters. All glory to our flesh, which infects us with the folly of birds drunk on that azure sky and the stillness of cats drows-ing in the pale gold that the sun pours in streams over the living-room carpet. While a lay brother worked manure into the black earth of the flower-beds, I longed to pay tribute to the morning coffee, to the bowl of ice water in which my senses splashed about, to my first cigarette, to the door opened abruptly upon a garden sprinkled with ashen light. But repelled by the insipid rustling of the forest, I turned and made my way back indoors. On the way, I invented faults with the food, with my mattress, with the very air I breathed, the better to excuse my precipitate return toward Christine. "A man shall not take unto himself his father's wife, nor shall he deprive her of his father's protection," the Bible says, or words to that effect. Regretting the twenty years that separated me from my mother, I thought:

One day, I shall find myself face to face with her corpse. And where shall I turn, then, if not to her, however dead she may be? If I know that I can never see her or touch her or speak to her again, not even at the end of the time it would take me, like the bird in the catechism, to grind down a steel sphere the size of a planet with my beak, then how and why go on existing?

Father Freeman's community had given me shelter for two months. I was passing through what is known as an adolescent crisis; in reality, the only moment when, having taken stock of his destiny, a man is tempted to follow his thoughts right through to an end. Afterwards, besotted with money or glory or comfort, he slaps his thigh and declares: "What a silly ass I was!"

The porter handed me an envelope, on which I recognized Christine's handwriting. I shut myself up in my cell and read the following message:

My child,

You are right, the proof of the absurdity of existence is that it took me forty years to realize that fact. But do not despair: the light is forcing its way little by little into my bourgeois brain. I can see how ridiculous it was to believe in such things as honour and honesty. For what did your father and I sacrifice our lives? For a lamentable error! Fortunately, you brought us to our senses. You cannot imagine the joy we feel at seeing you free yourself, flitting to and fro, scurrying about without a goal, for in this way we are made aware of the meaningless-ness of life. A fact, however, which leaves us indifferent, for we are already old and useless, no more worthy of respect than Camus' pestilential rats. I feel my heart drying up within me. What a relief! It's true that I am nothing but a mindless procreator. You should strike me down. The fact that I'm your mother shouldn't stop you. On the contrary, it would liberate you of the ancient conflict between good and evil.

You told me once that I ought to write a book. I feel such a revulsion of the absurd as it takes root in my soul that I am actually tempted to try. I would call it *The Void*, followed by a thousand blank pages. I hope you don't think I'm stupid enough to expend an ounce of energy on the void.

God? Since the seventh day of creation, he has been sleep-ing. Let's not awaken him. If the devil existed, I would say: may he take you all! But there is nothing: refuse, excrement, disembowelled rats, nothing but that. Like the young man in your fable, I want to sit by the door and wait, knowing I shall never pass through it

Your mother.

Whenever it was raining, I would remain in the house with Christine. Laughing, I would press my brow to hers and watch her two eyes merge into one. Not an eye but a sky, storms brewing about the black sun of the pupil, a deep well of fire and love over which slid the curtain of a mauve eyelid. And though I couldn't see her lips, I knew that my mother was smiling, because of the stars bound into sheaves in the depths of her cornea. Her dilated pupils sucked me in, pulled me deeper and deeper, in the direction of that distant, flaming, sacred thing that was herself.

Oh, Mother! Like a dying star, you closed the door of your eyes, and I wept alone on your shoulder. A wall was erected before your smile, and I bowed my head, for you were no longer there. In your absence, everything became black.

One day, when I return from school, you will inform me of

my father's death. It will be following a heavy snowstorm, and frost will lace the windows. You will raise me in your arms and the room will whirl like a merry-go-round. Or I shall awaken in the middle of the night, aware that you are watching me, about to probe my heart with your sharp nails. I shall think I am running toward the door and light, but I shall graze the window in passing and the curtains will part to reveal your livid face, barely distinguishable from the clouds licking the moon behind you, floating blithely along a river of dark molasses. And you will toss me into a cooking-pot with a narrow mouth, through which I shall be able to emerge only by slicing off my shoulders.

Following Guillaume's death, you went into a decline. You padded about the apartment in your eternal dressing-gown, your nose shiny from too much blowing, your head strewn with white hairs, your pale lips wearing a trace of a derisive smile, your neck with its rolls of fat. One evening, I appeared before you, wearing one of my late grandfather's suits, the sleeves falling to my knuckles. You broke into demented laughter, which still rings in my ears. The black cat fled, its tail and ears parallel with the floor. Taking me by the lapels of the jacket, you murmured:

"My poor child, you look just like a little girl in that suit!"

Edouard spent his days looking for work, returning each evening with a bouquet of flowers. Looking more Italian than ever, humming a popular tune, he kissed you and promised to buy you gowns fit for a princess. He was gay, too gay, for we were surviving on brewer's yeast and the landlord was threatening us with eviction. Guillaume's heiress, my skinflint of a grandmother, had cut us off.

I fear, Mother, I have nothing to say in reply to your letter. It is clear that the earth, with its tiara of stars, its yellow sun riding over its seas, its inky feet and its green throat, is not so beautiful when one lives in its mire; the earth does not sing when one is part of its vermin. But, for the pain that I have inflicted upon you, I shall masticate the dust in which yesterday's shadows sing; and, little runt that I am, I shall ask forgiveness of the flower for my offensive odour, and of the sparks of the wind for my slowness; little runt that I am, I shall embrace the earth and ask forgiveness of you, my beloved procreator.

More than anything, I would like to see you lying happily beneath the noon sun, a fly on your lips, twigs in your eyebrows, your streaming laughter dispersing the stars. See your fingers plunge at dawn into a pool of dew. I would like to take the place of the days and nights that slide beneath your skin and carry you beneath the earth. I would like, more than anything, to love you, all of you, right through to your bleached bones!

PUNCH AND JUDY

On the metal table sat a bouquet of artificial roses, their plastic petals glowing in the fluorescent light. Beyond the window, dark green hedges encircled a yellowing lawn. The odour of ether caused me to gasp. On the wrought-iron bed lay a body, its face wrapped in strips of gauze. Only the bloodshot, steel-grey eyes lent any life to what resembled the head of a giant match. At the point where it covered the mouth, the dressing, soaked with saliva, suddenly fluttered and there emerged the sounds of a raucous voice, trying to make itself heard over the rumbling of trucks outside the window. A brown intravenous tube coiled down from a bottle to the small of Suzanne's arm. Seated beside me on a leatherette couch, Edouard haltingly stuffed his pipe.

"The bastard had been drinking," said the voice. "It was his fault, and he didn't even get a scratch. Can you imagine how beautiful I'm going to be now, with my face torn open from ear to ear? He's given me an ear-to-ear smile!"

"*Maman*, why do you torment yourself like this?" asked Edouard.

The hands of the patient contorted on the sheet.

"It's the old man who'll get the last laugh. He didn't like to see me looking so young, called me a fool for having so many plastic surgery operations. A week ago, I could have seduced my own son. Yes, my boy, you would have been proud to dance with your mother. Now, when they get me out of this, I'll look like a doll someone has stitched up with thick black thread."

It seemed, however, that Suzanne's injury had given her a certain insight into her own behaviour.

"I'm not afraid of words, I've sometimes acted rashly."

She made a sign to Edouard to approach and whispered something in his ear. He paled, all but his nose, which remained red: he resembled a clown. He took a step toward me, then turned and moved in the direction of the door, kicking at open space in passing. A faint gurgling sound came from behind the gauze: Suzanne was laughing. I fell into step behind my father. As I was about to leave the room, she called to me. But there was a look of such malignance in her blood-stained eyes that I turned and hurried away.

Outside, darkness had fallen. Rain falling on rain, falling on nothing. Edouard stiffened and blew on his fingers. It made little difference to me that my grandmother and her lover had struck a tree and that the old witch was finally being obliged to sing to her own tune; but my father, walking sniffing at my side, looked like some poor kid who had struck his thumb with a hammer. For the moment, the only sound was the crunch of our shoes on the gravel.

"When I was young," he murmured, "a nun warned the girls who flirted too much that their hair would turn into steel wool. My mother can never be punished enough."

On the horizon, the black flames of the trees crackled silently into the star-studded sky. The wind scratched at doors, like a dog seeking admission. Suddenly, Edouard stopped before a long trench in the earth, probably destined for a pipeline.

"You see that hole?" he asked, his voice suddenly exalted, as if he had just had a revelation. "It's smiling. And do you know why? Because it's empty. And because, in a world of fools, perverts and overflowing graveyards, it's a funny thing to be empty."

And he reached into his pocket and removed a large, beige-and-white, checked handkerchief. But for that mourning Pierrot, there was a full moon that spun in the sky like a coin and life was a game of chance. For that Punch, captivated by what seemed to him to be his own grave and into which he would soon plunge, legs spread, hands clenched, hair dishevelled, there was a son who knew the way back home, to a gas fire belching smoke and a little mother waiting beneath the halo of the nightlight.

Winter. Space was as confined as in those little water-filled globes with their scenes of the Nativity and their cloud of white crystals that come to life with the slightest shock to create a simulated snowfall.

With the first frost, everyone in our household came down with a cold, which henceforth governed all our acts and thoughts. Edouard was always the first to fall ill: since his brothers had broken his nose, the slightest fever developed into a head cold. His eyelids swollen, his head enveloped in a cloud of vapour, he would lie in bed, moaning softly. In the middle of the night, we would hear him coughing and clearing his nasal passages, sometimes sounding like a trumpet, sometimes like a flute. We found his pink and yellow Kleen-exes all about the house, even on the kitchen table; and, everywhere we went, we inhaled the pungent odours of the medicines with which he rubbed and soothed and drugged himself. It was the beginning of the long saraband of aspirin tablets, thermometers anxiously held up to the wan light of windows, and periodic visits by the doctor, who brought the smell of the outdoors into the house on his wet rubbers. It was a period when each day was a little snowball melting in the dark palm of the night, when life became so bogged down we lost track of time.

I found it intolerable that I should be well, while my father was pampered by Christine. It seemed to me that my healthiness cut me off from the mysteries of a delightful cult, symbolized by mustard plasters and heating pads. So I took steps to alter my status: I walked about without shoes on, I plunged my head into snowbanks, I ran until I worked up a sweat then unbuttoned my coat and allowed the nails of the wind to tear mercilessly at my chest. Soon I began to shiver, my eyes and nose began to sting, and I gave voice to a triumphant sneeze. I had a cold, a real cold! I grew a shell about myself, I hibernated like the bears, I floated in the stuffy pod of my illness. In my overheated room, wrapped in cotton wool, I imagined myself in a cavern so deep beneath the surface of the earth that I could hear the roaring of the flames at the earth's core. My windows looked out, not upon the exterior world, but upon other, vaster caverns with strange fluorescent walls.

Boredom had the taste of a strawberry-flavoured syrup: we kept asking for more. Occasionally, I would open a comic book and in my brain—which, hitherto, had been content with brief excursions into the unknown—circus tents would spring from the earth and yellow rivers would unwind beneath a sky full of Chinese dragons. It took all of Christine's attentive, maternal care to quiten our dreams of troglodytes.

It was following his mother's accident that Edouard began to suffer from chronic sinusitis and refused to set foot outdoors.

THE BLUE ROOM

Following Guillaume's death, Madeleine lived on alone on a large estate in a suburb of Quebec City. Afraid of being robbed, she had an alarm system installed to protect the doors and windows. It was a house in the Victorian style, bristling with lightning rods and weathervanes. Two towers with bay windows flanked the main structure, to which were adjoined a coach-house sheltering an old limousine and a shed where the handyman kept the garden tools. A rough limestone wall encircled the grounds, which in the summer were flecked with beds of tulips and pinks.

With the years, my grandmother's face became more and more emaciated and her eyesight dimmed, while the hair of which she had once been so proud began to fall out. Since I enjoyed her favour, I visited her often, with instructions each time to ask her for money. She received me in a circular boudoir, decorated with old tapestries and extravagant knickknacks. The furniture exuded an acrid odour of lemon oil. On the walls, glittering in their ornamental frames, hung portraits of Guillaume, who seemed to be spying on us. With each visit, I was taken more and more into her confidence. Solitude weighed heavily upon her. After cramming me with sweets, she would ensconce herself in a deep armchair, her feet resting on a red pouf, and sip her coffee. Her smile led me to believe she had once been very seductive. She would paint glowing portraits of her former suitors, telling me how she had driven each one of them to despair. Her voice would become sprightly and her cheeks would flush. She often complained of the insensitivity of her late husband.

"He didn't know how to embrace," she would sigh. "But Lucien! Oh, what a dashing lad that was! Eyes as bright as boot buttons! And such a complexion! If he hadn't been a professional card player, I would have married him."

Thanks to her garrulous nature, I discovered that she had deposited her wealth in more than twenty different banks, under as many fictitious names: a ploy to foil the tax collector.

To combat her chronic insomnia, the doctor had prescribed sleeping-pills and advised her to take up smoking to occupy her leisure hours. However, watching her eat and fuss about, I had no doubt she would live to a ripe old age. Sometimes, on the pretext that it was late, she would keep me overnight. I was always given the room next to her own. The latter, with its indigo ceiling, its padded turquoise walls and its canopy bed, inspired me with a secret fear.

"How it would burn!" I thought.

Each night spent in that house filled me with dread, the odour of medications to combat rheumatism, the old books with their turned-down pages, the pairs of old-fashioned, gold-rimmed glasses—all these things bringing Guillaume stealthily back to life. As I slept, a cold draught would invade the room, the door would open and my grandfather would appear on the threshold, his hands thrust in his pockets, chewing a wad of gum. He never spoke.

"Get out of here, you old scarecrow!" I would yell at him. "Go let the worms finish eating out your brains!"

Without flinching, he would turn in his tracks and sink silently back into the shadows.

In Madeleine's absence, I once opened a padlocked chest, whose key lay on a dressing-table, and discovered a hand-written will, making me her sole heir. This was a discovery which I kept from my parents.

Autumn. One of my favourite pastimes was squeezing the pulp from the seed pods of the maple trees, which, as a child, I had called "propellers," because of the way they whirled when they fell through the air. The sidewalks of the Grande Allée were covered with them, along with bright scarlet and yellow leaves. Far from saddening me, the vicissitudes of the seasons filled me with joy, with the intoxication of sudden departures.

One day, I visited my grandmother to discover that she had exchanged her mourning outfit for a pink, tailor-made suit. A splash of rouge tinted her cheeks. Since our pantry was empty, I had come to beg $20, which, uncharacteristically, she handed over without a fuss. Then she clumsily lit a cigarette.

"Do you remember Lucien?" she asked. 'Well, he called the other day. He's given up card playing. He worked for 35 years for a loan company. Now he's a widower and retired. Like me."

My attention was caught by the tawny flash of a squirrel outside the window.

"Are you listening to me?"

"Uh . . . yes," I muttered.

"I met Lucien yesterday. He hasn't aged. Well, not much. He looked such a nobleman, in his corded velvet jacket and his silver-headed walking stick! He complimented me on my appearance. When I addressed him formally, he said with a smile that I had been more intimate with him in my youth. Then . . ." She took a deep breath. Intrigued, I nodded her to go on. ". . . he asked for my hand. He said we could make a new life together, he could think of nothing more delightful. He would sell his house in Montreal and we would travel."

Her rough hands trembled, keeping time to her toothless mouth, while her pale eyes shone. She was in love. I showed my disapproval of her passion with my silence. In all its cruel purity, the sky outside seemed to cry: "No hope for an old woman like you! Death is already at the doorstep!" My grandmother began to weep quietly, her head wagging foolishly.

"It's crazy, I know. What would your mother think? And my late husband?"

She dabbed away her tears with the corner of her spotted apron, then asked:

"What would you like for dinner?"

That night, I was awakened by the sound of an alarm. The room was stifling. I could hear a dull roaring on the farther side of the wall. *Fire!* I leapt into my pants and opened the door. The hallway was ablaze! Whirling about, I opened the window and crawled out onto the corrugated iron roof of the coach-house. Through the window of my grandmother's bed-room, I could make out the blue room invaded by thrashing tendrils of fire. The old woman's silhouette was etched for a moment against the crimson creepers, then the window broke. The beams collapsed. A thin wailing sound reached my ears, only to be drowned out by the sirens of an approaching fire-truck. Before leaping onto the gravel driveway, I thought I caught a glimpse of Guillaume down below me in the garden, standing beneath a thuja tree.

The inspectors concluded that Madeleine must have grown drowsy from her sleeping-pill and drifted off with a cigarette in her hand. As for the money . . . well, the fire having destroyed the dead woman's papers, it slipped forever out of our grasp.

RIDICULE

We had moved to Saint-Malo. Soon after our arrival, Edouard nailed a four-leaf clover made of plywood to the cornice above the balcony. At night, strangers crept up the outdoor staircase and scrawled insults on it. But my father didn't yield; he merely repainted the clover a bright bottle green.

Christine took a job in a department store. She was coming more and more to resemble Guillaume, especially when, tired from scrubbing the floors, she would sit with one hand pressed to her heart. I found her one evening stretched out on the couch, as motionless as a corpse. I placed my fingers against her lips to be sure she was breathing. Without moving a muscle, she said: "I'm dead." And the water dripping from the leaky faucet in the sink went *ping! ping! ping!* in time to her words *dead! dead! dead!*

At first, I had been intimidated by the city. But I soon learned that all that concrete and steel was no more important than a pebble polished smooth by the sea. From a fear of going under, man has fabricated all those glass stalagmites and brick factories with his blind, sticky hands. What a farce! In the public squares, the blades of grass seemed to smile, thinking of the day they would creep back over all those grey avenues, covering them like a soapy froth.

"Patience," they seemed to say. "Our time will come."

Meanwhile, I observed my fellow human beings as, one by one, they were caught in the trap.

(It was only yesterday, wasn't it, that the flowers budded? So what are those dead leaves doing crackling beneath my feet?)

Seated at the kitchen table, I watched the black clouds that the wind was blowing my way. Christine sat opposite me, sipping scalding coffee. Then the snow began to fall, big, soft flakes that glowed in the light of the naked bulb on the balcony. Edouard was pacing the floor, muttering invectives against the Jews and the Communists. I wanted to speak to Christine, but the words were caught in my throat. The snow falling outside the window, my chest rising and falling with each breath—all these things were living and dying for no reason.

Edouard accused God of betrayal. His eyes resembled two open wounds. I couldn't imagine what nightmares caused him to cry out as he did at night, what forebodings made his features suddenly dissolve in the middle of a conversation. He had always had difficulty expressing himself, but from the moment he realized that my knowledge in certain matters exceeded his own, he made only the most pedantic pronouncements; and these, as often as not, were incoherent. He floundered about in a sea of outlandish ideas, while I waited for him to open his heart to me.

One evening, after he had filled my plate with crêpe suzettes, he began to get playful, simulating an awkward left hook. I reared back, my arms waving wildly, as he struck me on the shoulder. Seeing red, I knocked him to the floor. In falling, his head struck the bureau with a loud crack. He lay on the floor without moving. For a moment, I thought: "I've killed my father." I saw myself suddenly as a condemned criminal, stripped naked, my eyes glazed with pain, being flayed alive by my knife-wielding executioners. A long strip of flesh, attached at the heel, hung from my right leg, the exposed muscles and nerves gleaming like an inflamed vagina.

Edouard gripped my arm.

"What's the matter, boy?"

But not even the sound of his voice could pull me from the nightmare in which I struggled, like a diver entangled in sea-weed, running out of oxygen.

"I've told you not to horse around with Pierre," said Christine, removing her coat. "Look at him! He's in a daze!"

The murder of Edouard would have been the fulfilment of an inadmissible dream, like the one that impelled me at times to climb on a chair and pass my head through a noose, standing on the edge of the chair and dreaming voluptuously of the one false move that would transform me instantaneously into a hanged man who had suffered from bad taste.

Since my father was made of crystal, I would almost certainly break him one day, however inadvertently. Like a piece of fine china, he would smash on the floor. Then I would be swept up in the grey arms of the wind, which would carry me to the four corners of the horizon.

The lake had steep, slippery banks. The machine-gunning of raindrops on the metal roof of the porch suddenly drowned out the gurgling of the stream that ran past the house.

"Do you want a drink?" asked Suzanne.

Perched on a bar-stool, she eyed me maliciously, her blond hair tinted a garish hue by the red and yellow lights of the big electric star that hung on the wall, an acquisition from Edouard. In her dress with its pink flounces, my grandmother resembled a Chinese fish lying motionless at the bottom of a bowl filled with exotic knick-knacks. Her beauty was not perceptibly diminished by the scar that ran across her right cheek or by the loose flesh quivering beneath her arms.

Edouard had gone for a drive in Suzanne's new car. I had refused to accompany him, on the pretext of not wanting to leave our hostess alone; but, in fact, I wanted to talk with this woman, whose vices and cruelties fascinated me. She had haunted my childhood like an ogress, her physical absence from my life (this was only our third encounter) only serving to increase her legendary status. Surrounding her like an aura were my eight uncles, several of whom had turned out bad, in contrast to my father, who was girdled in morals. Dazzled by the luxuriousness of her setting, the bottles of alcohol that suggested incredible orgies, I longed to inspire Suzanne's admiration and love.

She moved haughtily toward the bay window, one hand on her hip, her head held high. Whirling about, she asked:

"How do you like me? I haven't lost my figure, eh?" She set her glass on a table.

"You're fifteen years old. A young man looks good at that age."

I swallowed a mouthful of alcohol. Outside, the storm had broken. The lake no longer shivered but sent high, strong waves crashing against the shore. Suzanne seized me by the elbows and drew me to my feet.

"God, but you're tall!"

In my half-drunken state, her words buzzed in my ears like a swarm of angry bees. She began to unbutton my shirt. The sight of Edouard's star, clicking on and off, on and off, caused me to break into laughter, one of those irrepressible bursts of hilarity, whose object is existence itself, glimpsed for a moment as a ridiculous, little thing swaggering like a loud-mouthed braggart.

I drew back, irritated by her caresses, ready to flee. But the couch, the books, the paintings, all these things sucked me in like quicksand. Tangled up in the purple drapes, I could see my own reflection in Suzanne's eyes, a goblin imprisoned in a glass bottle.

She threw back a full glass of whiskey, then, articulating each word carefully, said:

"Poor child, you're all out of breath! You're covered with sweat!"

Like white grubs flecked with little curly black hairs, her fingers ran over my left hand, the sharp nails digging into the flesh.

"Look! Your flesh is turning red! You're bleeding!"

But I felt no pain, only a sense of disgust as I watched that big, flaccid spider spin its web from my larynx to my lungs, from my heart to my vital organs, slowly wrapping my entrails in its silk.

"Now, I want to know why you laughed a moment ago," she said, lashing at my cheek. "Was it because of my scar? Or were you afraid I'd take you to bed? I only go for men! Little boys, I gobble up!"

And, like a snake hypnotizing its prey, she gazed deep into my eyes, her thin, bony torso undulating slowly before me. Swollen by the downpour, the stream hissed and gurgled as it rushed beneath the kitchen, which was built on pilings.

"Why?" she repeated, "Why?", backing me against the refrigerator.

A door slammed. I heard my father's voice:

"It's raining cats and dogs out there! I drove the car under the carport but I still got drenched!"

"Don't come in here!" yelled Suzanne. "You'll only mess up the carpet! Wait till I bring you your slippers!"

I slipped out onto the balcony and turned my face up to the rain, letting it cool my fever. Forget! I must forget! Like those clouds and those pines, for whom the words love and hate would never be anything but displaced air; and who, a century from now, would have called back to themselves the few billion men at odds with eternity.

During dinner, Edouard, intoxicated with noble sentiments, praised the family and maternal love, even quoting several poets on the subject. His eyes misty, he recalled his childhood and the dreams he had once cherished of becoming a great doctor. Suzanne went him one better, declaring that her fortune left her indifferent to such matters, that only art could console her now. They took their leave of each other with many kisses and promises of future reunions.

In the bus that carried us back to Quebec City, Edouard turned to me and said:

"You could have kissed your grandmother goodbye. I'm

82

sure she was upset by your coldness."

I thought of Guillaume's pale, frank eyes when I had gone to bid him farewell. "Are you going away?" he had asked me. Yes, I was going away, setting out on a long voyage, while you, Guillaume, were just finishing yours. But you were right: no farewells, no tears. In this life, only silence is suitable to the occasion; and, elsewhere, there is nothing.

AN OBSTINATE NOISE

At home, in Saint-Malo. The outhouse, surrounded by a fence of fir planks. In the rear wall of the kitchen, the black rectangle of a doorway with peeling paint, which became yellow when Edouard lit the lamp in his room. An immense apartment, with six rooms, including a living-room that doubled as a dining-room. Walls oozing soot and dust. The sash windows, covered with designs I had traced on their grimy panes, resembled Byzantine mosaics when the lights of passings cars embellished them with green, red and orange discs. In the living-room, where I slept, chunks of plaster fell regularly, nibbled by invisible mice.

For a few months, Edouard had looked for work, but now he paced the kitchen floor, a pipe in his mouth, until late at night. This incessant moving to and fro was simply one more sound added to those of the foundations being worked on by the cold, the scurrying of termites and other vermin, and another persistent, almost inaudible sound that I was never able to identify. On certain evenings, in the disconcerting silence following the passage of an ambulance, it resembled the sifting of sand in an hour-glass or the slipping of wet tires on pavement; at other times, it was like the jeering laughter of a crowd heard through a thick layer of cotton wool.

Day broke with the pale face of an assassin and the viscous wheeling of bats. The tenements across the way began to fall thick and fast behind the curtain of immobile flakes. Christine got up, and I smelled the mingled aromas of coffee and toast. She fussed about the old salmon-coloured table, looking a little more wasted each day. Only her eyes retained a trace of her former beauty, flashing in the sockets of loose, ashen flesh, beneath the cloud of fine, white hair.

"My shift doesn't end till nine o'clock," she would say, using the English word *shift*, as she knotted a scarf about her head. "Don't wait supper for me."

"What kind of talk is that, Mother?" asked Edouard.

"It's the talk of the place where *I* work!"

My father nervously chewed his moustache and, as if to avenge himself for this stinging retort, declared:

"I don't recognize you anymore, Christine. Why don't you buy yourself a low-cut dress and dye your hair? You could use it."

The door slammed behind her. Withdrawing behind a screen of fragrant smoke, Edouard went back to dreaming of his inheritance.

The spider that spins webs that the dawn turns iridescent; the black wasp that lays its eggs in the entrails of a paralyzed scarab, so its larvae will have something to feed on; the scorpions, the cockroaches, all those insects that implacably and mindlessly reproduce themselves, which were distilling their venom millions of years before our arrival on this planet— today, they are fattening, gaining a firmer hold. The cities emit the dark glow of anthills. Man has never belonged by right to himself; the slightest distraction, and he slips back into his black armour and equips himself with a thousand pincers. You leave a friend, and return to find a termite.

Since the evenings were long, we spent them devouring one another. A fluted lampshade cast rays of light over the living-room floor. Christine picked Edouard to pieces, heaping insults upon the male sex. She was disintegrating before our very eyes, her legs scored with varicose veins. Huddled in an armchair, my father raved.

Her hands clasped firmly over her abdomen, my mother

said sweetly:

"Instead of sitting there daydreaming, why don't you go and sweep the streets?"

"If only you would give me a little encouragement! If only you would say, '*Papa*, you deserve . . .' "

"*Papa?* You'll never take the place of my father, you fool!"

Her wrinkled face flushed, she sat fuming with rage, while Edouard turned more and more in on himself. Suddenly, a shadow of a smile passed over her face and she leaned over my father, pressing him to her breast. During the mating process, the female praying mantis devours the male, beginning with the brain, while he fertilizes her ovaries, releasing his grip only when his entire body is consumed. To nibble away the soul takes much more time, but Christine's jaws ground tirelessly, while her stomach slowly digested the prey.

THE RED VAN

A clump of artificial daisies trembled on her hat. She blinked her eyes, as a young blond man in a parka called to her:

"Hey, Grandma, I bet the old men you sleep with have to crank themselves up to get going!"

The prostitute nervously fingered the imitation pearls of her necklace. With her faded face, her heady perfume and her rumpled dress, she had come in here to eat, perhaps also entertaining the hope of latching onto a client in the smoky pub. To draw attention to herself, she had plastered rouge on her cheeks.

"Ugly old caterpillar!" persisted her persecutor, encouraged by a concert of laughter.

She gazed into space, her hands lying flat on the table to hide their trembling. Her legs twitched. Despite the stiffness in her joints, she strove to still the trembling of the chair and the ashtray, which had been drawn to her attention by some banal remark, but she succeeded only in further betraying her agitation and confusion. She smoked too slowly and with too much application. And what was she hoping to prove by constantly sticking her tongue between her teeth like that? Thirty or more pairs of eyes ogled her. Someone poked his neighbour with an elbow and snickered:

"Look at the old tart!"

Gazing at her steaming plate, she seemed to have given up the prospect of eating, for fear the fork might slip from her fingers; or of leaving, for fear she might stumble and fall. Crossing her arms over her chest and closing her eyes, she capitulated, abandoning herself to the curious gazes of the onlookers, who undressed her with their eyes.

At that moment I became her. Instead of a suit, I found myself wearing a sweat-stained dress. I felt the fatigue of so many hours spent on my feet, the disgust with my unclean, ageing body, the stifling weight of a thousand looks.

Then I became the young blond man, then a handsome old gentleman, then a boy. Moving amongst these strange personalities, I discovered with a shock their common identity and the insignificance of my own singularity. The room was large, small; filled with gaiety, sadness; dark, bright. The seats . . . but none of that mattered, neither the colours nor the sounds, in the light of this strange force that multiplied them to infinity.

"Will they ever stop mocking me? . . . And I have no more money."

"Poor woman, what a pity! Still, I'd go to bed with her in a pinch."

"The $1 boiled beef. And a 50¢ beer."

"I've had enough, I've got to get out of here. . . . Let's hope my parents have gone to bed."

These final reflections were mine. I had ricocheted about the room, dropping back finally into the snare of myself: that malicious young blond man whose drunkenness and hatred I felt surging once again through my veins. He rose with a smile, pinched the arm of the tart and, pulling up the zipper of his parka, passed out into the cold. By some sort of ironic metamorphosis. I had found myself absorbed by the very one that, only moments before, I had most scorned.

I haunted the clubs and, to betray my boredom, betrayed others. The drinks drunk, my mind and my memory burnt out on the lights and the music, I sat dazedly contemplating my left index finger as it rested on the tablecloth. Above the moon of the nail, the flesh was red. The material felt rough against the ball of my finger, a sensation beneath which began the inexplorable depths of cotton and wood. I fell, a prisoner of matter, lacking light and oxygen. When I reached the bottom of myself, I was in a region devoid of hope. My hand existed, opening or closing to caress or strike, but it lay outside that region at the bottom of myself where only three poppies survived: Nothing: this word played havoc with my solitude. I was twenty years old, I should have some substance, some weight. Voluptuous memories, with which I tried to arouse myself; others, more bitter, that left me with the illusion that in suffering I had learned something. Edouard, Christine: names that buzzed in the shadows like the drugged wasps of boredom. What did I have to do with them? Or, for that matter, with these customers? A feeling of such revulsion swept through me that I wanted to address myself to an inhuman god, confess my shame at belonging to a race whose extinction was long overdue.

Man? A pair of tortoiseshell eyes attached to a sack of entrails and bones. A puppet lodged in a cranial cavern, itself containing another, and so on, *ad nauseam*. . . . Our century has simplified things, decreeing that there shall be only one puppet, endlessly reproduced, rigged out in a top hat, a morning coat and dark glasses. From the moment of its birth, it sits on a folding chair, gazing through the portholes of its eyes. The spectacle varies from one human bathyscape to another, giving rise to the unfortunate impression of diversity. But, just as the divine, imbecilic scriptwriter, short on invention and Creation, makes a botch of a film entitled *The End of the*

87

String Beans, the marionettes greet this long-unacknowledged truth: *I, you, he* do not exist, only *they* think and act. Off with the masks, then! And let *them* embrace before the curtain falls!

I wandered aimlessly through the deserted streets. We shall never witness any more beautiful spectacle than this snow falling beneath the milky globes of the streetlamps, and that lighted sign suspended like the crest of an emerald wave above the heads of the passers-by. I stopped to relieve myself in the darkness of an alley. Before me, a black steeple rose gently into the blind sky. There was no moon, only a yellow halo about the perforated bronze cross, a sign of the times in the heart of the unfolding centuries, grinding, cutting, polishing each stone, each face.

I returned home, more drunk than usual. Edouard was waiting for me in the living-room. Fearing his reproaches, I fumbled out of my overcoat and said:

"I missed the last bus, I had to walk home."

"What do you think of me?" he asked timidly.

I shrugged.

"I'm sleepy and, if it's all the same to you..."

He pressed his fingers against his eyes.

"You can't imagine what goes on in this old noggin of mine. I'm so tired I could lie down right there on the carpet. I've failed at everything. There are times I tell myself that my death would make everything so much easier for you and your mother."

Despite anything I might say to the contrary, these notions filled me with scorn.

"Go and hang yourself, then. Isn't that what everyone does, sooner or later. Either with a rope, or a woman, or alcohol?"

"Your sister has left."

"Good for her! You despised her!"

"And what about you, my boy? Do you love me?"

"Passionately! I should have thought that was obvious!"

Suddenly he leapt for the window and smashed it with his

fist, then, zig-zagging about the room, hurled himself at the furniture and threw the dishes to the floor, a strange rattling sound escaping his throat. He didn't seem to notice the stream of blood that was splattering the carpet. Breaking into a sweat, convinced that he was about to strike me, I sank onto the sofa and shut my eyes. When nothing happened, I opened them again. He was standing in the middle of the room, gazing in bewilderment at the blood pulsing from his wrist.

"Ah, that feels so nice!" he said. "So nice! In a short while, I'll be nothing but a few coagulated drops of blood between the floorboards. It's less painful even than losing a tooth or a fingernail." His entire body was trembling. He went on in a faint voice: "If I'd known it was this easy, I wouldn't have waited so long."

The room was growing cold, the snow blowing through the broken windowpane. I had the impression I was looking at Edouard through a plate-glass window or from the far end of a long tunnel.

It reminded me of a dream: following a long trek on the steppes, I had come to the edge of a precipice, below which, alone in an ochre desert, sat our house. I knew I would never be able to reach it unless I leapt into open space. My father's death agony, which was taking place before my very eyes, did not surprise me: I'd been awaiting it since the day of my birth. I was about to go to his aid when Christine suddenly flew into the room. She was wearing a nightgown, beneath which I caught a glimpse of her naked body, the skin grey and wrinkled. She wrapped her arms about her husband and led him to the sink. I heard the water gush from the tap, the tearing sounds of gauze, a voice pleading:

"Oh, my darling, my love, please don't start this again!"

A very old, very painful knot broke somewhere inside me. In the kitchen, two sobbing strangers embraced: a man with salt-and-pepper hair and an overweight woman who had cast me one night onto this slope down which I was slipping faster and faster, moving toward a fetid ditch filled with tadpoles and eels. I had nothing in common with my parents. The wind blew gently, like an old man sitting beside the fire.

Christine, who had slipped into a tattered housecoat, appeared suddenly in the doorway, a look of hatred in her eyes.

"You would have let him die, wouldn't you?"

And, without waiting for a reply, she turned and vanished. I searched for a record album to cover the broken windowpane. I could feel the bile rising in my throat. Then I noticed, outside in the alley, the little red van, the one that I knew would never fail me, its motor slowly idling. The moonlight sliced through the clouds like a knife through living flesh.

THE GAME AND THE CANDLE

She stood before the steamy mirror, grimacing, then, lowering herself into the scalding bath, opened the case and extracted a razor blade. With a quick slash, Suzanne cut her left wrist to the bone.

"The first time I've menstruated in years," she thought.

The water grew red. With her right hand, she reached out and turned off the tap. Sixty seconds: too long. A whole minute, and still nothing had happened. The hands of the watch, which lay on the checkered tiles, wove invisible bonds about her body as it struggled against eternity. In a few hours, a servant discovered her, dead.

Four mica lanterns spread a wan light over the excavations. The sounds of the pickaxes and my uncles' curses were evocative of a construction site. They were burying my grandmother, whose suicide prevented her from being laid to rest in a Christian cemetery, at the edge of the lake, on the fringes of the fog-shrouded forest. I hunched my head down into my shoulders and took the path skirting the cottage. A magnolia leaf brushed my face. When I reached the yard, I flopped down on the doorstep, which was sheltered from the rain by a small roof. Before me flowed a stream, over which arched a little bridge.

A branch cracked and the figure of a woman emerged from the mist to lean against the railing of the bridge. She was wearing a bell-shaped hat with a feather, and a dress that fell to her ankles. I couldn't see her face, but I noticed she had an old-fashioned fox fur slung about her shoulders. Standing with one hand on her hip, she suddenly broke into harsh laughter. It sounded just like my grandmother. Then she turned and moved toward the yellow rectangle cast on the ground by the light from the bathroom window. I sank back into the shadows. The ghost suddenly tore off its hat and stamped on its stole. A young girl with sharp cheekbones stood before me, her arms raised to the falling rain. It was my cousin, Ginette, the one I had once dressed up as a princess and defended from bandits.

Suddenly, I heard my father's voice from the farther end of the grounds:

"Pierre, it's your turn to dig. Your uncles and I are going inside to get warm."

I emerged regretfully from my hiding-place. Ginette started and stretched one hand in my direction, but I slunk behind the corner of the house. Passing before the verandah, I heard Edouard bellow:

"You shouldn't drink like that, Armand! You're showing a lack of respect for the dead!"

And a drunken voice replied:

"I don't give a damn about her, I spit on her . . . All right, 'Ti-coune, all right, don't get worked up over nothing! We'll erect a pink marble stone over her grave!"

I seized the shovel, which lay on the coffin, and leapt into the grave. I could hear the waves splashing on the shore. Her soggy dress clinging to her body, Ginette suddenly appeared above me:

"Why did you run away? Did I scare you?"

I shrugged.

"I was wearing Grandma's clothes. You know how I like to

dress up." Squatting down, she went on in a low voice: "You look so unhappy these days. You used to smile, but now I can see their fever in your eyes. You'll pass it on to your children."

In a rage, I sank the blade of the shovel into the clay.

"Listen to them," she continued. "Producers of mass misery. And the rain this evening is so gentle."

"I detest them!" I exclaimed.

"Your father, too?"

"I can't stand the pity he inspires in me!"

She nodded, as if she had anticipated my reply. An owl hooted in a nearby tree.

"The werewolf of our ancestors," she said jokingly.

Was it that demon, or was it Suzanne rotting there at my side, who had condemned me to fear, to the kingdom of ice, to the millenium? Anger caused me to flare up at my cousin's fickleness, her cardboard optimism.

"Do you still have hope, then?" I cried. "Take a good look at what's awaiting you! Metal tubes will replace our limbs! You'll dig a rut between the factory and the house! As an afterthought, the doctors will cure you of that contagious disease, life! It'll be day in the middle of night, it will simply knock you out with its beauty . . ."

"There's the truth of love . . ."

"We'll have our truth when we become radioactive!"

Playfully, she tried to take the tool from my hands.

"It's deep enough."

I pulled the shovel away violently. She staggered and we fell together into the muddy hole. She moaned. Her mud-splattered hair looked like the roots of a giant flower. The lanterns cast their ghostly light over the lacerated flesh of the earth, in which we squirmed like maggots in a wound. A mass of low clouds covered the sky. I raised my cousin's skirt and began to caress her belly. I wanted to cram her full of mud, to sink with her beneath the earth, our two rotting bodies fused forever together. I made what is called love, but what I call death.

No-one will extract any descendants from me. The blood-thirsty vivisectors and the brilliant inventors will pullulate elsewhere than in my seed. I am disconnecting myself. Let the current of humanity pass through another wire. "You will become as numerous as the sands of the sea," said a famous stage director; in other words, none of you will ever amount to anything.

Her face streaked with mud, her dress torn, Ginette sat quietly weeping. The verandah door slammed. I leapt to my feet.

"Quick!" I muttered. "My father's coming this way!"

We ran into the underbrush, where I had parked my car. Once safely in the front seat, I watched as Edouard staggered about, wiping his mouth with his sleeve. Armand must have struck him.

I apologized to my cousin for having abused her.

"At least, you didn't lose your head," she replied. "I won't become pregnant, that's all that matters."

I turned the key in the ignition and the milky light of the headlamps spilled over the figure of Edouard, who was shovelling earth into the grave.

"Look!" Ginette exclaimed. "He forgot to put the coffin in!"

But is the hole really empty? I thought.

THE ROLE OF FIRE

Just as a person emerging from a dungeon is blinded by the light, so I suffered unspeakable torments from the moment of my encounter with Ginette. We slept together in a narrow, metal cot, the sheets of which exuded the same close, acrid odour I had often smelled on my parents' bed. On the farther side of the glass door, black chimneys studded the mauve sky. One arm covering her breasts, the other thrown above her head, my cousin was sleeping. I raised her left eyelid to discover the trap into which I had almost fallen. If I rejoined her there, in the fortress of her eyes, if I seeded the land with her lips so that their echo should speak of love, the forest in which I now trembled would become her hair, the world would grow tame. Her germination complete, Ginette would then crush me. Like Edouard—and, before him, Guillaume—I was the crystallization of a refusal to exist. Misery flowers only in a hot-house; in the open air, it withers and dies. Remembering the abbey near Boston that offers refuge to weary travellers, I silently dressed and made my way to the terrace of the Chateau Frontenac. The ferry to Lévis was fighting its way across the ashen river, whose waves beat out the seconds, the centuries. The rising sun, flanked by a wall of purple clouds, was like a gateway opening into a marvellous garden. A few pedestrians hurried by, the sound of their heels echoing on the boardwalk, as in the vaults of an empty palace. I returned home and quietly packed my bags. Edouard and Christine were lying side by side, asleep. In the black orifices of their gaping mouths, death was building its nest. Death, that friend who wrongs no-one, especially not those it chooses to strike! On the bus that carried me toward the monastery, it struck me that, for the first time in years, my parents had looked happy.

What will you do, you presumptuous creature, when your father begins to slide backward down the thread of life, like a drowned man whose gaze grows dimmer with each passing hour? Will you go in search of the bluebird of happiness for him? His slack face, his decomposing features: poison darts speeding my way! Beneath what strange suns will you reap the harvest of hope? Look, Father, I'm climbing on the roof-tops, I'm swinging on the banana of the moon, I'm playing a violin strung with my own entrails!

Would everything be drained, then, tainted, turned to brine? But still they erect their towers, whose glow on certain summer days they cannot endure? Soon, the planets will be acquainted with the grandeur of man. Applaud, Father, dance with them about the mass graves of the world's fools and reactionaries! God, how hollow the earth sounds beneath our

94

diabolical heels! A rain of gold and carnival masks on the cosmonauts, who pass beneath the *arc de triomphe* of a giant sausage.

Quick! Where did I put my foolproof little salesman's kit? *Monsieur mon père, s'il vous plaît* . . . He's not here? But I wanted to sell him a sheet-iron star, a supply of miraculous orange juice . . . or my latest invention: life.

The bed is large and soft. The acidic odour of sweat. A small room, a honeycomb cell drenched in a sweet golden light, enclosed by the secret passages of dreams. You go to bed, you reach out and latch onto an idea, you set fire to it, you rub your face with its ashes. What time is it? Midnight, already? You killed two minutes with a single idea. You will begin again tomorrow. Seated in the bus, you will nibble at a thought, you will masticate it in the street. Once back at work, there will be no more need to rack your brains. You see: living is not complicated, not difficult at all! It's like chasing butterflies in a ricefield. Your reflection trembles in the light of the setting sun. The water-flowers open their petals, as you dart like a seal across the flooded countryside. No shortage here of noctuelles, sphinxes, phalaena, exuding their poisonous cyanide. Dead memories affixed with pins to a card: something to gather dust.

But Edouard is no longer listening to me, so I pack up my merchandise, I stop speaking, I smash my internal tape-recorder. Step right up, ladies and gentlemen, see the most taciturn man in the world! Every day, at three o'clock, he mutters . . . What? Louder! . . . he wails: *Life is a case of farcical diarrhea.* Then he resumes his seat in the tent, which reeks of sick monkeys. The spectators hurl insults at him. Meanwhile, in Vietnam, the bronze Tang-To ceases contemplating the third stone on the left wall of his little temple and douses himself with gasoline.

Forgive my sudden departure, Father. I could no longer tolerate the knowledge that night flows through you with a perpetual, ear-splitting clamour. As a result of heredity and instinctive sympathy, I was coming more and more to resemble you. Farewell, I leave you in the care of Christine, who will watch over you like a burning candle. Here, in this monastery, I have recovered my reason (which wears the robes and helmet of Minerva), my joy (which flows from the eyes of a woman yet to be conquered) and my death (which will come with loud oaths and a building of funeral-pyres).

As if to put an end to these reflections, Father Freeman has come to inform me that I must leave this place, handing me the letter from Christine that I had been awaiting with the impatience of a wolf tearing at a ewe, anxious to taste the hot, steaming flesh of the heart. To the devil with her! My beloved mother, with the voice and the designs of a siren. She wants to drag me down with her. I shall not grieve over these ridiculous ashes. This way, Pilate, with your basin and your white towel.

My child,

You must excuse the harsh tone of my last letter. I thought then: let the whole thing end with a curse! But disgust quickly yields to indifference. Time subdues us with repeated blows of its spurs and its whips. The hours pass at a walking pace; the years, at a full gallop. How is it possible that the accumulation of so many interminable seconds can result in something as ephemeral as life?

Edouard has aged a great deal since his mother's suicide. One day recently, he visited Vincent, his father, who found God only knows what pretext not to attend the burial. The old man was lying on a *chaise longue*; at his side, his concubine and her "cousin," impish grins on their faces. Vincent looked uneasily at your father, as if fearing a scandal. When Edouard went to the kitchen for a beer, the pimp followed him, as impudent as ever, and when your father made some innocuous reference to the smallness of the room, the parasite replied:

"On the contrary, it's very large. But, it's true, you're not very bright, are you? A fact which seems to have escaped no-one but yourself."

You can probably imagine your father's reaction. He gave the man such a drubbing, I had to step in and plead with him to stop, I thought he was going to kill him. And then he turned on his father, accusing him of having provoked Suzanne's death. He was shouting at the top of his lungs, as if he wanted to destroy the old man with his words.

In the train that carried us back to Saint-Malo, he sat with his teeth clenched all the way. But he is forgetting now. He has transformed your sister's room into a sort of solarium, in which he grows potatoes. If you only knew with what love he waters the plants and fertilizes the earth, with what care he prepares me tasty little dishes when I return from work! The other day, I stupidly took offense because your father seems to have found happiness. But that's all that matters, isn't it?

Your mother.

PS   My father's grave is only a stone's throw from here. The other day, I discovered rats burrowing amongst the gravestones. They had dug a tunnel all the way to the coffin. I filled it with smoke and water. A waste of time. They flee through their network of subterranean tunnels and, even as I water my pansies—you know how your grandfather loved those flowers!—those damned rodents defy me again and again. The little bastards can't wait to sink their teeth in me! But I set traps for them, I impale them, I crucify them. If I had the courage, I'd cook them and eat them with a white sauce. This little war consoles me: I have not yet become one of them.

COMING SOON

The supreme tactic consists of disposing your forces in such a way as to make them seem without form; then, the most astute spy will not be able to track you down and the wisest man will be helpless against you—Sun Tse.

CHAPTER ONE

I

Intermission. Jack gulps down two more valium tablets with the cold dregs of a cup of coffee. A man is standing in front of the restaurant window, cradling in his arm a teddy bear that he won in the shooting-gallery at Belmont Park. He climbs onto the bus; when it departs, the sidewalk is deserted. Soon, the patrons will begin to emerge from the movie house. For a moment, their silhouettes will be etched against the two giant posters on the building's façade, one of which depicts the head of a tyrannosaurus with long, studded jaws, the other, the slender prow of a drakkar. The headlights of cars will flash on in the parking-lot, casting on the dentist's house across the way a series of luminous circles, which will stretch into ellipses and disappear.

Jack takes a mint from the saucer beside the cash, then crosses Boulevard Gouin and enters the movie house. A padded wall of imitation leather, surmounted by velvet curtains, separates the lobby from the auditorium. He climbs the stairway. In the mirror covering the wall at the top of the stairs, he watches his reflection approach him, like a tilt shot taken with a zoom lens.

The heroine of the film is weeping. "Erik is dead," she says over and over. Jack knows the scene by heart: a black pigeon has settled on one of the fortress' towers, provoking Brünnhilde's grief; this, the pre-arranged signal that Erik the Viking has fallen upon misfortune. But how could this bird have covered the distance between America and Norway in a single night? How could you kill yourself so rapidly that the reflection of the act would be delayed to the point that you would not observe yourself die?

His torso bare, Jack rewinds the second reel of the feature-length film by hand, while in the other projector the final reel slowly unwinds. Wiping his face with his shirt, he raises the volume of the cabin's loudspeaker and leans toward one of the windows. He is watching this film for the tenth time, a repetition that deprives the scenes—skulls staved in with axes, kisses exchanged in the light of the setting sun—of all dramatic or narrative value, purifying the universe before consigning it, when the lights are turned on in the cinema, to the empty expanse of a bare white screen, 1000 square feet in size.

Unknotting her blond braids, Brünnhilde leans out of an aperture in the tower, high above the glittering ocean that stretches between the dark bands of sky and cliff. "Are you still thinking of him?" murmurs her maidservant, who is preparing her mistress' bed. Meanwhile, far away, in a gulf of what will one day be known as America, Erik stands on the narrow prow of his drakkar and addresses his oarsmen: "We have found neither gold nor cattle here, but only tribes of hostile people. I propose that we leave to others, more numerous or more insane than we, the business of settling this land." The Vikings strike their shields with the flat of their swords as a sign of assent. Now, Erik will return to Norway, to Brünnhilde, and will punish the traitor by hurling him over the cliff. *The End.*

Pivoting on his stool, Jack unfastens the clasp holding the curtains. He has never seen such a badly made film: the pistons beneath the platform are clearly visible during the rolling of the boat in the storm at sea; the waves that spray the crew spout from hoses manipulated by technicians; the jungle in which the Vikings make camp contains a polar bear and an elephant; the Indians, red circles painted about the navels of their distended bellies, wear ostrich feathers and throw spears with aluminum tips.

Jack moves to the other projector and lifts the hood: the lantern fills the air with a blinding, white light, more impenetrable than the shadows that shroud the hall. Turning a dial, he extinguishes the lamp. The two carbon filaments whose contact produces the light are almost totally calcified, but they will hold out for another four or five screenings.

Back in the lobby, the usher and cashier having left for the night, Jack sits slouched in a chair that he has placed at the end of the centre aisle. Little by little, the darkness between the screen and his gaping eyes begins to shift, to undulate slightly, giving birth to a myriad of forms. Suddenly, a match is struck in one of the first rows and the glowing tip of a cigarette moves up the aisle toward Jack. He flips the switch.

II

"Bravo!" I exclaim. "You didn't slip up on a single change!" Then, to forestall any questions, I quickly go on: "No, I wasn't sleeping, I was waiting for you. I hope I didn't alarm you. I'm looking for your brother."

Jack drops a coin into the candy machine and removes a chocolate bar.

"It's been a long time since I saw Bernard, Monsieur. . . ?"

"Jean Jolin."

His chin cupped between his thumb and index finger, he gazes at me over the top of his round glasses. Somewhere behind us, the seat of a chair rises with a thud. A second person steps into the light. He's wearing a string tie and tight pants, which go well with his beak-like nose and the hair slicked back on his pointed skull.

"Denis works here as a projectionist," says Jack. "In the daytime, he has a more dangerous job: he dies before the cameras."

"The boss means I'm a stuntman," says Denis, a note of irritation in his voice.

Jack stares at me as if he were trying to recall where and when he has seen me before.

"I need some air," he says. "The ventilation system in the cabin isn't working properly, I've been breathing carbon dust all evening."

"You want to be careful," I reply, moving toward the exit. "That could dull your wits, even leave you feeble-minded."

Outside, I find myself subject momentarily to the malaise that results from emerging suddenly into a three-dimensional world, with roads along which you can move, which do not rush to your encounter and suck you into a vortex of immobility. Feeling the earth fall away on all sides of me, I close my eyes to clear my head of the sudden dizziness.

"What do you want with Bernard?" asks Jack,

Complying with my invitation, he and Denis follow me out to the parking-lot, which is filled with potholes and covered with broken glass and that rises steeply at one end to a taxi stand, from which can be heard the crackle of radio-phones. I rummage among a heap of papers and clothing on the back seat of my Mustang and emerge with a file folder.

"This is a copy of the script your brother commissioned from me and which I submitted to him last fall. I'd like to know if he has begun filming it yet."

"I haven't the slightest idea," replies Jack.

He lowers himself onto a swing at the top of a high mound, its red-and-white candy-cane poles glowing faintly in the lamp-light. He makes several revolutions, causing the chains to grate against the rusty cross-bar, then sits and gazes at the big house across the way, a legacy from his father: the façade of artificial stone, the doorstep partially hidden by little fir trees planted in pots and arranged to form a balustrade, the frosted windows at ground level of what was once the dentist's office.

"Did you like the film?" he asks. "Totally insignificant, don't you agree, that tale of the Vikings? It was the last thing Bernard commissioned for our cinema—his last will and testament, you might say."

He raises his feet from the ground and lets himself spin slowly about.

Then he asks me about the script. Omitting certain details, I explain that Bernard wrote to me on several occasions about how it was his intention to film a war before it actually took place. He would use obsolete army tanks, whose cannons had been plugged to prevent them from being fired. The action would be filmed in various vacant lots in Montreal, the sites of demolished buildings. As he saw it, the only technical problem would involve unplugging the cannons and replacing the little deposits of black powder normally used to simulate the impact of bullets with real cartridges. He realized, of course, that this would necessitate introducing, into the very heart of his creation, the death that could not be simulated, a feat that would at the same time allow him to disappear. When I asked him about the actors, he informed me that he himself would play the lead role.

"I just returned last week from a trip abroad," I conclude.

Denis stops kicking at the turf with the toe of his boot to ask:

"Why don't you join us for a drink? Then you can explain to me how it's possible to make a war film without using a single trick shot."

Unlike a policeman or a private detective, I do not enjoy the privilege of bringing all my suspects together in a dramatic confrontation. And now I find two of my principal witnesses falling out of character. Once again, chance is rearing its ugly head. Here we are, in an unpredictable, irrelevant scene, retracing our steps along Boulevard Gouin, insignificance insinuating itself on all sides; first, in the form of an old woman who greets us, a cardboard cone of half-eaten cotton-candy clutched in one hand, the spoils of an excursion through Belmont Park; and now, in the guise of the heavy-set owner of a tavern called *Le Rendez-Vous des Sportifs*, standing outside his establishment and calling: "Hey, Jack, when are your dirty movies going to arrive?" Because I am exhausted, I cannot stem the flow of all these swarming intrusions, which find their concentration in the beer parlour of a Cartierville hotel, where Jack wends his way among the square tables, their shiny black-and-white surfaces covered with water stains. And the presence of a whore in one of the rear booths, next to the one in which Jack and Denis have ensconced themselves, completely paralyzes me. From a scriptwriter, I have become a character in search of a plot, one that will be too complex for me to make any sense of it, much less order my movements.

"Did you watch the film carefully?" Jack asks me.

"I saw only the end."

"Like me, then. Denis replaced me for the first 60 minutes. This is the sixteenth time I've shown that film. And, you know, each time I'm struck by the resemblance between Erik and my brother. When the actor isn't speaking, when he's photographed from a certain angle, I have the impression he's going to step through the screen and walk right up to me."

On the shoulders of Jack's shirt are two vertical, rust-coloured stripes, left there by the chains of the swing. Denis is slouched in the corner between the imitation leather seat and the bare concrete wall. He mutters something to the girl in the next booth. She gazes at me, her eyes wide with incredulity, then breaks into laughter.

"Is it true you're a dirty old man?" she asks.

The Adam's apple in Denis' throat bobs up and down as he gulps his beer. The waiter's towel swishes over the tabletop, which is covered with ashes and peanut shells, then is rolled back around the sleeve of the white jacket with gold buttons.

"Another dry martini," says Jack.

Denis reaches out and seizes the prostitute by the hair, twisting his fingers into her frizzy mop and forcing her head and torso out over the aisle. A boot makes contact with her ribcage, and she drops to her knees on the floor. Clinging to the back of a chair for support, she rises and disappears into the crowd.

"You must excuse Ginette," says Denis. "She has a lot of heart but not a brain in her head. . . . I find it a little strange that Bernard didn't mention your script to anyone."

"Have you had any word from him since he left?" I ask.

Jack shakes his head. He lifts the plastic pick from his glass, pops the olive into his mouth, chews the pulp and spits the stone under the table. His teeth glow in the black lights overhead, two rows of tiny fluorescent bulbs revealed by the fixed smile on his face. In the same way, it is possible to pick out each speck of dandruff in his hair.

"And his silence doesn't worry you?"

"Did you sign a contract with my brother? I'll look for it in his papers. Do you live in the vicinity?"

"No, in the country. I have no telephone."

"You'll have to call me, then. But, you know, I'm not responsible for any committments my brother made. You'll have to take up your case with his associates."

Suddenly, all eyes are on Mimi, the Goddess of Love, standing before a fake backdrop of cacti and haciendas, vivisected by a 500-watt bulb that is trained on the stage. The band, *Les Sensuels*, breaks into a voluptuous tune. Mimi disrobes and stretches out on a couch, where she pretends to make love with a customer, whom she has silently invited to climb onto the stage and nestle up to her breast; but in play only, as is made unequivocally clear by the bouncer to the naïve young man who leaps onto the stage and drops his pants. Her body, tinted pink and blue by the footlights, is suddenly shaken with spasms. Against the blasting of saxophones and guitars, Jack's voice echoes in my ear:

"I hope Bernard never returns."

III

It is a few hundred feet from the Commodore to the highrise where I live, on the shore of the Rivière-des-Prairies. I park in the underground lot. No chance that way of anyone noticing my Mustang. A slight feeling of nausea, then the elevator stops at the tenth floor. The caretaker hasn't collected the trash from the metal containers at the side of the doors: the hallway stinks. I cross through the studio apartment and step onto the balcony, whose walls guarantee my privacy. The wind must have changed: the notes I made this afternoon are blown up against the railing. While I'm retrieving the sheets and returning them to the table, using a cup as a paperweight, I hear the bell signalling the closing of Belmont Park for the night. Before looking at a planet through a telescope, you must focus it by using a nearby object, a streetlamp or a tree. I use a lighted window down below my observation post. As I adjust the lens, I see a jumble of letters, which gradually become clearer and finally materialize as the front page of a newspaper tacked to the wall of an empty room. Because a telescope always shows things upside-down, I have difficulty making out the words. Triumphing over this decoding problem gives me more joy than discovering Saturn and its ring, millions of kilometres away.

The lead story concerns a coup d'état. But someone turns out the light before I can learn who has seized power, the masses or the armed forces. I remove my eye from the telescope and gaze down at Jack's house, waiting for another light to come on. Nothing. The only lights in the entire neighbourhood are in the fairground, where the merry-go-rounds, the ferris-wheel and the roller-coaster will remain illuminated all night, along with the wrought-iron lanterns on the walls of the Commodore. Instead of the traditional marquee, the movie house has an almost vertical, false shingle roof, the only decorative addition to this oblong box that resembles a cavern and that was once endowed with a steeple. It was the grocer who told me that M. Rivest, Jack's and Bernard's father, bought the old church and transformed it into a showplace. I leave the telescope on its tripod and go in to bed. The mastery of the visible and the invisible, daylight and darkness: therein lies the entire art of war. He who possesses this secret, even though dead, may return to life, knowing exactly when to make his appearance and when to disappear.

Every evening, Jack takes two sleeping-pills and falls into a deep sleep. In the morning, he cannot remember his dreams. It is probable that during the day he repeats the events of the previous night. Which may explain the feeling of *déjà-fait* he experiences while searching Bernard's room. No obvious clues: no letter with its revealing postmark on the envelope, no appointment book with its tell-tale names and dates. But yesterday's encounter with the scriptwriter, with all his awkward questions, has whetted his curiosity. Why did Bernard try to conceal all traces of his stay in this place? The only thing he left behind is this apparently insignificant sheet of newsprint, its giant headline proclaiming the successful overthrow of a government by the armed forces, an object that would arouse no suspicion if it hadn't been placed in such a conspicuous position in a room whose walls are otherwise bare. Was there not an important clue in this article: "About 9 PM yesterday, a ship was blown up. The cause of the explosion remains unknown. The drama unfolded on the ice-field off the coast of Labrador. Helicopter rescue forces despatched from Sept-Iles failed to discover a single survivor of the 27 men on board *The Swan*. In addition to its regular crew, the ship was carrying a team of film-makers, come to shoot scenes for a feature-length film set in seal-hunting country." While folding the sheet of newsprint, Jack notices that the paper has yellowed and dried. He examines it more closely and discovers that it was published nearly ten years before and that the official stamp of the Bibliothèque Nationale is affixed to the back of the page. Why would Bernard have wanted to steal this document from the archives? Instinctively, Jack comprehends that he must not let himself be outstripped in this investigation by Jolin, who appeared out of nowhere, demanding information about some unproducable script. In fact, he finds the appearance of this man more disturbing than the disappearance of his brother. He goes to the living-room and burns the sheet of newspaper in the fireplace. Then he leaves the house.

An old man, wearing a tight suit and a deliveryman's cap, is pounding at the basement door.

"Are you Dr. Rivest, the dentist?" he demands.

"The office has been closed due to a death," replies Jack.

"So take down the sign," retorts the man angrily, rubbing his chin.

Jack crosses the street, enters the *Chez Paulo* restaurant and takes a seat at the counter.

"Your baby has a beautiful tan," the owner is saying to a woman, who stands with her infant tucked beneath one arm, recounting her recent trip to Florida.

"Oh, that's his natural colour."

She flips through a pornographic magazine then returns it to the rack, while the owner turns to a big man and asks him to open a bottle of ketchup for her. Jack spits out the bits of paper napkin he almost swallowed with his hot dog. Suddenly, it starts to rain, driving the customers outside at the picnic tables indoors.

Denis lowers himself onto a stool, muttering:

"The scriptwriter's car is parked in front of the movie house."

The two friends take up positions behind the window, peering through the intricate designs of a Coca-Cola sign at the black Mustang parked on the street.

"You take over tonight," says Jack.

He realizes that he will shake off Jolin only when he discovers the true nature of the relationship between him and Bernard.

CHAPTER TWO

I

I carefully draw the curtains. In the dim light of the infra-red lamp, the negatives soaking in the developing fluid begin to come clear, revealing the scenes I photographed earlier with the telephoto lens. One hand shading her eyes from the sun, the other on her hip, a young woman stands gazing at Jack, who is passing a watering-can over a row of pumpkins. I profit from the moment of respite afforded me during the drying period to switch on the tape recorder. The man gasps for breath as he speaks, as if he'd been running. Footsteps crunch on gravel, followed by a groan. In the distance, a dog bays. "Look, I'll explain to you . . . What's that? No, you can tape my words if you like, it doesn't bother me. I didn't think I was doing anything wrong when I gave the reels to Jack. . . ."

I had waited patiently, knowing the little man would use the rear door of the film company's offices, since he had parked his car in the yard. Now, seated on an upended garbage pail, he rubbed his sore shins. In his desire to destroy the clues, Jack was actually drawing them to my attention. So he made a mistake in burning that sheet of newspaper shortly after I had succeeded in decoding it. The little man, one of Bernard's associates, told me what I already knew: the film made on board *The Swan* had turned up nine years after the shipwreck in a fishing shanty at Sept-Iles; the ice had preserved the negative along with the cod. Following that discovery, which had been treated by the press as a simple coincidence, Bernard found himself wondering about the validity of the official version of the event. He reopened the inquiry on his own, hoping to prove that someone had placed an explosive device on board *The Swan* before returning to shore and hiding the film in the fishing shanty. At the same time, he embarked upon a more complex task: the development of the 50 reels of film left behind by the assassin, and the selection from the thousands of scenes and images of those that would correspond with the plot of the narrative submitted to him by the script-writer. "I helped him with the editing," continues the little man's voice. "But none of it made any sense. We could have constructed at least a hundred different plots from those images. But he was obstinate, fanatically obstinate. Of course, our attempt met with failure. So when Jack came for the reels this morning, I figured he'd simply fallen under the spell of his brother's obsession. . . . It's strange, I have the impression I know you. What are you carrying in that case? Surely, it's not . . ." I switch off the tape recorder. I have developed the last of the negatives. Encumbered by her long, tight skirt, the young woman braces herself against Jack's shoulder as she climbs onto the train. I must see what I can find out about her.

II

When will the TYPEWRITER be delivered to Jack? Inadmissible survival of the paleolithic: the use of a pen and a brain to compose a text that should unfold at the speed of light. The content of the thought matters less than its rapidity; it must spin, whirl, like the nucleus of uranium at the moment it is transformed into pure energy. The consciousness must become radioactive, play havoc with the geiger-counters, destroy everything within a radius of 100 miles. There was a time when the words were not inscribed within reality, but contained it. Now, the projectors of the Commodore flash images at the rate of 24 per second, and Jack's pen drags across the page, despite the countless cups of coffee he has drunk. At the moment, nothing but this monotonous murmur, whose sense remains hidden behind a constant play of interchangeable questions and answers. No-one has ever heard Jack. The words have concealed his voice, which speaks no known language, receding into the neutral space of that sheet of paper within which it seeks the magic formula, the abracadabra capable of recreating the universe.

III

Eleven o'clock. No-one at the cash. I slip into the Commodore. The carpet on the stairway muffles the sound of my footsteps. The corridor, broken in the centre by the door to the projection cabin, leads on one side to the women's toilet, on the other to the men's. A customer is standing before one of the urinals, buttoning his fly. He steps up to the mirror, passes a comb through his greasy hair, then wipes the comb on his sleeve to remove the flakes of dandruff caught between the teeth. I pretend to consult the telephone directory, which is hanging from a chain beneath the wall phone.

Once alone, I check the stalls and discover one of them to be locked. But the space between the tile floor and the bottom of the door is large enough to allow me to crawl inside. It's a closet, used to store toilet paper and disinfectant, and contains a pail with a wringer-attachment and a mop. The cleaning lady won't be here till morning; I run no risk of being discovered, I have the entire night to conduct my search of the Commodore. At regular intervals, the urinals flush automatically. Suddenly, I hear Denis' voice:

"Are we going to sit down below? All right, I'm coming."

Apparently, I'm not the only one who has decided to remain after the closing. The muffled sounds of a conversation reach my ears from the ground floor. I venture out of my hiding-place and grope my way to the projection cabin, which is plunged in darkness. A faint light glows beyond the sound-proof window, behind which I take up my position. A 16 mm. projector has been placed on a folding table in the middle of the centre aisle. Denis and Jack emerge from a room beneath the stage, each carrying a stack of metal boxes. These must contain the reels that Bernard attempted to edit and that came into his brother's possession last night.

Framed by the velvet curtains, the screen is flooded with light, a large luminous square with rounded corners. A series of numbers in reverse order flash on the screen. These are followed by the traditional group photo of cast and crew standing with arms linked; behind them, a number of sailors waving their toques. Panning to the left, the camera focuses on a copper plaque on which is inscribed the name of the ship: *The Swan*. A young man, crouched on the ice, is rubbing his nose with his mittens. Of the figures grouped before the camera on that December day, not one survived; according to newspaper reports, that is, for Bernard was convinced that an as-yet-unidentified assassin was lurking in their midst.

Jack stretches out in his chair and, leaning toward Denis, mutters something in his ear. Denis stops the film and points to the young man in the mittens. The two friends enter into a lengthy discussion. In order to hear what they are saying, I emerge from the cabin and move half-way down the stairway.

"I tell you, it's him," Jack is saying. "He's aged, of course, but look at the nose, the chin, the eyes: they all give him away."

"And I tell you I don't believe in ghosts," replies Denis. "I saw Jolin, I shook his hand: he's alive! How could he have been part of a film crew that was blown sky high?"

"He knew my brother had conducted an investigation. He wanted to find out whether I was taking over from him; the script was merely a pretext. Perhaps he wanted to destroy the film."

The position I have adopted, squatting on the stairway, is rather uncomfortable. My legs are growing numb. If they decide to come up here, I doubt if I could move fast enough to hide. There is a long silence, then Denis says in an exasperated voice:

"You can finish your detective story another day, I'm going to bed."

The door slams behind him. Jack remains alone. I return to my observation post.

His chin resting on the back of the seat in front of him, Jack scrutinizes the screen with the eyes of a wary hunter. Since the images are not accompanied by a soundtrack and are repeated almost indefinitely, with sudden abrupt shifts that have no apparent connection with what has gone before, the only way they can possibly be viewed as scenes, or segments of a plot, is with a liberal dose of imagination. They remind Jack of those psychological tests in which the patient is asked to explain what is suggested to him by random splotches of ink. Any number of foreign elements threaten repeatedly to distort the interpretation, to render the distinction between fact and fancy all but impossible: flaws in the film, sudden changes in lighting, errors made by the cameraman. At least Jack has succeeded in identifying Jolin. The latter is entering a kitchen, in which the table has been pushed up against the wall next to a cast iron stove. A number of old people, seated on chairs arranged in a circle, are clapping their hands, while, in the middle of the room, young people dance a jig. Jolin's eyes, outrageously made up, angrily follow the movements of a young woman dancing with the villain. His lips mouth threats, perhaps an accusation. The dancers draw back and the heroine takes refuge in the arms of an elderly man, probably her father. The two adversaries stand face-to-face in the centre of the room, defying each other. Dodging a blow from Jolin, the villain strikes him square in the face and knocks him to the floor. The others break into laughter, including the girl, and point derisively at the loser. A love triangle, Jack mutters to himself. But to what extent were the actors, Jolin in particular, playing roles? Suddenly, he hears a noise, like the snap of a bolt or the release of the breech of a gun from the direction of the stairway. He seizes the projector and swings it about, focusing the beam of light on the lobby. A shadow moves across the front of the candy counter. He hesitates a moment, ready to throw himself upon the intruder, then realizes his error: the shadow is created by the film itself. When he shifts the beam of light back upon the screen, he sees Jolin, rifle in hand, moving toward a pen in which a number of huskies are fighting over a hunk of meat.

When the scene shifts back to the ice floe, wan beneath an overcast sky, Jack returns to his seat, seized by the absurd fear of finding himself prisoner of that vast, deserted landscape. Suddenly, as if by magic, the illusion heightened by the long period when nothing was happening, the ice floe is swarming with men pulling on a cable attached to the prow of a ship. Viewed in silhouette, the vessel is struggling to free itself of the ice, its two chimneys belching smoke that quickly mingles with the low-lying fog. The propellers, invisible despite a close-up of the rear of the steamer, whirl frantically, churning up the water in the ship's wake. The captain waves his arms and barks a command. The sailors drop the cable and take refuge behind the snowbanks, while three of their comrades open a steel box, remove sticks of dynamite and attach them to stakes, which they drive into the ice all about the vessel. The villain, almost unrecognizable in a fur hat pulled down to his eyebrows, surreptitiously shortens the wick attached to the explosive devices, thus rendering them highly dangerous for the one assigned the task of igniting them. Then he moves toward one of the groups that has taken shelter behind the snowbanks and speaks to Jolin. It is clear from his gestures and the expression on his face that he is challenging the man whom he earlier vanquished with his fists (or will later vanquish, depending on the as-yet-undetermined order of the scenes).

Jolin tears the stick of dynamite from his adversary's hands and advances resolutely to plant it in the spot indicated by the captain, who is leaning on the ship's rails. He lights the treacherously shortened wick and quickly retreats, but the explosion catches him unawares before he can take cover. His body is thrown into the air by the impact, then drops back, a disjointed figure covered almost at once by a shroud of pulverized ice.

The villain smiles, but only for a moment, for Jolin suddenly struggles to his feet, apparently suffering not even a scratch. Stunned, he shakes himself and once again finds himself the object of general hilarity.

Jack is irritated beyond words by this highly disorganized film, strewn like a dream with apparitions too rapid for his brain to record. Because there is no logic to their sequence, the individual scenes are quickly forgotten. He cannot remember which reels he has already played and which still remain to be viewed. As for Jolin, he no longer recognizes him in this hairy actor whose facial features seem to be constantly changing. He raises his eyes once again to the screen, but with the indifference of a passenger on a train to the landscape passing by him outside the window.

The sheet of ice upon which the two adversaries are standing suddenly floats free. By the time they've recovered their balance and caught their breath, it has drifted too far from the floe to allow them to jump to safety. Now, they are lying side by side on the ice, while the snow slowly covers them up. At dawn, when the storm has passed, Jolin struggles to his feet. All about him, as far as the eye can see, lies the open sea. He shakes the villain and orders him to his feet, for any prolonged immobility in this cold will be the end of them. They walk in a circle, one behind the other, as if, despite their extreme weakness, they were stalking each other; as if, on this melting raft which is slowly shrinking beneath the blazing sun, only their hatred for each other kept them going. Jolin, triumphing this time because of his greater stamina, keeps the villain moving, not out of pity for the man but because each time he pulls him from his fatal torpor with a kick or a slap, he is prolonging his own existence.

It seems to Jack that the actors who performed these scenes must have been out of their minds. There were no trick shots, neither during the dynamiting nor on the ice floe during the storm. Maybe it had been the director's intention to kill them all. No doubt it was this that had caught Bernard's fancy, for he had often said that film-makers should not stage combats but record the real thing. And did Jolin, struggling now in a scene that fluctuated constantly between fiction and reality, really survive the explosion of *The Swan*, or was he still performing on a screen more fluid and intangible than that of the Commodore?

V

Jack has left. I don't think he was able to make any sense of what he saw. Only two things could lend any meaning to that iconographic chaos: a careful editing or an instinctive grasp of the truth, like that which allows an archer to find his target, guided by an acute perception of danger. But unaware that the images offer him any threat, including the ones depicting me on the ice off the coast of Labrador, Jack has allowed himself to be carried beyond the climax without even recognizing it. I move up the centre aisle and take one of the reels he screened from its metal case, on which a seal bears the inscription: *23 cutter helicopter photos—before sunrise.*

The scene is so brief it almost escaped me, too. I play it backwards. Time is suddenly reversed: the explosion gives birth to a ship, which slides backward into its own wake, its chimneys sucking in smoke. I stop the projector. Someone is clearly distinguishable on the bridge of the ship near the steerage. I rerun the scene, this time in slow motion. The sailor, miniscule in the distance, walks toward the prow, then the three explosions light up the screen.

To leave certain places, it is necessary first to reach them, to persuade yourself that a certain real distance separates you from them. Otherwise, endowed with their enormous gravitational pull, they will take possession of your mind and slowly crush it to a pulp. The place I wanted to visit was *The Swan*, during the moments prior to the explosion; in particular, the bridge of the ship, where, standing with my back to the squall and saluting the captain in the nearby steerage, I must have been able to hear the hull breaking through the ice. Then, suddenly: a flash, a fiery breath that lifted the body into the sky.

The frozen, dismembered corpses were discovered by the helicopter rescue team within a radius of 1000 feet of the wreck. They piled them pell-mell into mailbags and flew them back to Sept-Iles. Since it was impossible to identify many of the victims, they were buried in a mass grave.

Unless, that is, it failed to snow that day, in which case death must have come slowly, atrociously, while their clothes caught fire and they rolled about on the ice floe before throwing themselves into the icy water. But that is something I shall never know, though I might relive it a thousand times, in every possible variation, in my imagination.

And now, gazing at this shot of the hero, a bearded, scowling man wrapped in a muskrat coat and holding the reins of a team of huskies, I am troubled. This scene provokes no feeling of loss, only the absurd hypothesis that these blurred, black and white images gave birth to me, that I once existed on that screen from which, by some strange twist of fate, I have been catapulted temporarily into reality, here to remain until such time as I can regain my original place, standing behind that dog team, rifle in hand, waiting for the villain to fall into my trap.

I unfold the blade of my pocket-knife. When the film is sliced into tiny fragments, which lie curled at my feet, I leave by the emergency exit, for Jack has locked the front door.

VI

The last Viking poet encountered the gods only in his dreams, and only then in grotesque forms. The people looked upon him as mad and drove him off with stones. And they were right to do so.

Night after night, the dream is repeated, risen from the depths of some celluloid Middle Ages: dressed in a green silk doublet, Jack rides on a series of escalators to the roof of a skyscraper, where a sort of fortress or keep rises several fathoms above all the modern structures that surround it. With the aid of a rope ladder, he climbs onto the battlements and discovers, in the heart of Cartierville, ten or more other towers similar to his own, each inhabited by a prince in fine raiment. Jack understands that these are the turrets of an immense vanished wall, one that must be reconstructed by razing the city, tearing up the asphalt and the concrete, then relaying the turf and the thick green grass, upon which his companions will resume their jousts, as in olden days, before stands full of noble young ladies and frail damsels, and a canopy-covered throne upon which the king, his sceptre resting on his knees, drinks from a golden cup. But, invariably, at this moment, Jack senses the presence of someone behind him. He whirls about, though not fast enough to stop Bernard from leaping upon him and hurling him over the edge.

CHAPTER THREE

I

When I introduce myself as a journalist, no-one bothers to check my identity. According to the dossiers that I consult, Bernard made only one documentary film in Quebec. The young archivist at the film library leads me into a dusty room, where rows of closely ranked metal shelves hold an assortment of antique illusion machines: a kinetoscope from the time of the Lumière brothers, a fixed-plate chronograph, a Marey photographic gun. The latter catches my attention, because of its name and its strange resemblance to a firearm, ready to kill at the rate of ten images per second. Why have investigators, in real life as well as in fiction, shown so little interest in iconographic murder?

The archivist places the reel I have requisitioned on the projector, whose operation he explains before leaving me alone. I switch out the lights. Thousands of tiny particles dance in the beam of light trained on the portable screen. The musical score drowns out the sound of the fan. The credits end with the name: Bernard Rivest. Then there is a close-up of a map of the Atlantic Ocean. A line travels from the west coast of Iceland to the southernmost tip of Greenland; according to the commentator, this is the route taken by Erik the Red, son of Thorvald, to escape his pursuers, in the year 981. A second line indicates Leif's voyage, four years later, from the colony founded by Erik, his father, to Vineland, the present-day Newfoundland. A third, dotted line skirts Labrador, enters the Gulf of St. Lawrence and ends with a cross at Anticosti Island, the spot at which researchers, working from specific geographical references in the sagas, have placed the last stand of Thorvald, brother of Leif and second son of Erik the Red, during a battle with the Algonquins.

The archaeologists have made camp somewhere on the sandy shore of the Bay of Sept Iles. In a quadrilateral formed by cords attached to stakes, they excavate the soil with trowels and pass it through a sieve. A family of Montagnais stands silently observing the white men, who pause from time to time to slap at mosquitoes or to reach for bottles of beer from a portable cooler. Facing the camera, wearing jeans and a short-sleeved shirt knotted beneath her breasts, a young woman—the same one I saw the other day with Jack—responds to questions from an invisible interviewer:

"My name is Julie Nantel. I've been coming here every summer for the past three years. The rest of the year I teach history at the CEGEP in Longueuil and analyze the results of our findings." She rubs her sunburned nose and gnaws her lower lip. "Of course, we've found more than containers of preserved food. There are human bones and fragments of steel at least a thousand years old. Everything points to the fact that a battle was waged here between the Indians (close-up of the face of a Montagnais) and the Norse explorers. We hope one day to construct an exact replica of a Viking ship and repeat the voyage of Thorvald from Greenland." She smiles wryly at the interviewer. "That would make an excellent subject for a film, don't you think?"

I stop the projector. A green blind covered with a network of fine cracks is flapping gently against the window pane. My actions at this moment are prompted largely by uncertainty. Because of the constant intervention of chance, the only thing I can count on anymore is a sort of inner clarity, trusting it to lead me to the truth, to the settling of old scores. That is why, against all logic, I decide to bring Julie and her excavations marching onto the drill ground.

II

Thorvald was preparing for a crossing with a 30-man crew. Leif, his brother, was offering him assistance and advice. The voyage to Vineland passed uneventfully. When they arrived, they dug in for the winter, surviving mainly on fish. In the spring, while the ship was being repaired. Thorvald took a light skiff and departed on a reconnaissance excursion. The country he discovered was very beautiful, with white sand beaches running from the forest down to the open sea. There was no trace of human life, but on an island they found a field of corn. The following summer, they navigated westward in the drakkar. At one point, a storm drove them up against the coast, after having broken their keel on the reefs. Thorvald went ashore with his men. When he saw the size of the trees, he said: "I like this place, I shall build my home here." As they were returning to the boat, they saw what appeared to be three mounds moving along the beach. They approached.

They were canoes, each carried upside-down on the heads of three men. Thorvald took the strangers captive, all but one who escaped by sea. They killed the eight prisoners, then climbed a nearby cliff. On the farther side of the bay, thin plumes of smoke rose into the sky. Exhausted, they lay down to sleep. Suddenly, they were awakened by a loud voice: "Thorvald, take your men and leave this place. If you hope to escape death, climb into your boat and depart this land at once." At that moment, a flotilla of canoes could be seen headed in their direction. Thorvald said: "We will make a wall of our shields to defend the ship but we will not attack." They employed this tactic, and, for a long time, sustained a rain of arrows. Finally, the Skraelings withdrew. Thorvald asked whether anyone had been wounded. The reply was no. "I have a wound beneath the arm," he said. "An arrow has passed between my shield and my breastplate and struck me in the armpit. Here it is. I fear the wound may be fatal. You must leave this place at once. Carry me to the spot where I wanted to build my home. Perhaps my words will come true. I shall take up my residence there for a time. Bury me with a cross at my head and another at my feet." Greenland had been converted to Christianity following the death of Erik the Red. The crew obeyed Thorvald's orders. They raised sail, wondering what they would tell Leif upon their return.

III

Julie stands hunched over the sink, wringing her hair, while Jack massages her back. Following the corridor from left to right on each floor, then descending the diagonal staircase to the floor below, they make their way to the ground floor of the caretaker's lodge, which has no elevator. Since this route reminds Julie of the movement of eyes over a page, she looks vaguely for a meaning in the splashes of soot and trickles of moisture on the plaster walls. At Central Station, they climb into the train bound for Cartierville. Now their faces are reflected by the ceiling lights in the window of the coach as it picks up speed in the Mount Royal tunnel. The bulbs beneath the arches on the opposite track flash by monotonously, and Jack finds himself imagining reality crashing through the windows in the form of an assassination attempt, annihilating all the black-clad businessmen hidden behind newspapers opened to the financial pages, only to instantaneously resurrect them, identical in appearance but moving in the opposite direction, back in the direction of the city. The only things that really exist for Jack are those that can be destroyed; never has he loved Julie so much and never has he experienced such a desire to annihilate her. She sits gnawing at the knuckle of her right thumb. Her blue-black hair, held in place by two hairpins inserted beneath the ears, frames the pallor of her oval face. The lights of the station where they stop momentarily twinkle between the two grassy embankments.

"When Bernard lived with you," Jack asks her, "did he ever introduce you to a scriptwriter by the name of Jean Jolin?"

"I thought we'd agreed not to talk about your brother," replies Julie, removing her earrings. "We were going to act as if he'd never existed."

Jack replies that circumstances oblige him to take an interest in the past, despite his promise to put all those things behind him. He finds himself in the position of having to defend himself against someone from another age, someone who is attempting to re-ignite ancient conflicts, an interference with the past that threatens to aggravate the slightest flaw in the texture of the present.

"Instead of shedding light on the mystery," he adds, gazing at the telephone poles as they flash by on his left, "he suppresses any clue that might lead to their solution. He's like a policeman turned inside-out. By rendering certain facts forever inexplicable, he multiplies the possible crimes and reduces to zero the chances of apprehending the guilty parties. That's why I suspect him of having destroyed the film I watched, because there was a chance I might piece the story together. He wants to obliterate any clues that might lead us to my brother. And in playing havoc with my memory, with the order I have lent to time, he is attacking me directly."

Jack smiles and kisses Julie's damp hair, to which the shampooing has lent a salty odour.

IV

For a long time: conflicting winds, fog, the sail lowered, the vessel adrift. The men were asleep on the deck, wrapped in sealskins. They knew that death would be like this, except that space would be bereft of memory. Leif, son of Erik the Red, was searching for the tomb of his brother, Thorvald. He had a calf and a heifer on board, as well as a supply of seeds, oats and wheat. He planned to found a colony somewhere up-stream on the shores of the great river. The fog lifted. Without realizing it, Leif had been skirting the shore. Two of his men failed to move when he ordered them back to the oars. Death had carried them off. Weighted down by their coats of mail and their weapons, they sank straight to the bottom of the river. Leif found the sheltered bay where Thorvald had first touched shore. He disembarked and, for three days, explored the coast. But the two crosses had disappeared. So he engraved on a rock the following words in the runic alphabet: "May you long enjoy the tomb." Then the drakkar continued westward.

Leif had to wage many battles. He did not dare to spend the night on shore, for fear he and his men might be massacred under the cover of darkness. He decided to return for the winter to the dwelling he had constructed near the tomb of his brother, Thorvald. But Gudrid and her husband, Thorgeinn, along with about 40 of their men, had occupied the place during his absence. So Leif said, "I don't have enough men to dislodge you. We'll settle this matter before the People's

Assembly in Greenland." And, far from the sea, he built another dwelling on the shore of a lake.

Winter came. At Leif's instigation, games were organized. Soon, quarrels broke out between the two groups. The people shut themselves up in their respective dwellings and stopped visiting one another.

The following spring, Gudrid rose one morning and dressed, but she did not put on her shoes. Wrapping herself in her husband's cape, she made her way to Leif's dwelling. She stood for a while on the threshold without speaking. Leif was awake. He asked Gudrid what she wanted. "I'd like a word with you outside," she replied. They sat on the trunk of a fallen tree. "How do you like this country?" she asked. "Very much. But I dislike the antagonism that exists between us. I do not believe I am responsible for this antagonism." "You're right. And so if you will exchange your boat for mine, I shall leave this place, taking my men and my cargo of wood and furs with me." Leif agreed and Gudrid returned home. In getting into bed, she knocked against Thorgeinn, her husband, and awakened him. He asked her why her feet were cold and wet. "I paid Leif a visit," she said angrily. "I wanted to buy his boat. But he struck me and abused me. If you don't avenge me, I shall leave you."

Thorgeinn ordered his men to take up arms and they raced to Leif's house, where everyone was still asleep. They took the men captive, binding them and shoving them outside. As they stepped into the open, Gudrid had each prisoner killed.

Once the men were all dead, there remained the women. No-one wanted to kill them. So Gudrid said, "Give me an axe." One of her men obeyed her. She attacked the five women. By the time she had finished, not one of them was left alive.

Later, Gudrid said, "If we make it back safely to Greenland, I shall kill anyone who tells of what happened here. We shall say they decided to remain in this country."

V

The conductor punches the tickets. New passengers replace those who have disembarked. The train runs between rows of duplexes, in the kitchens of which are revealed a series of tableaux, frozen by the speed: a man's hand raised before a woman to caress or to strike; a fork lifted to a mouth; a little girl suspended in the air above a skipping-rope. Julie closes her eyes at the very moment these scenes take shape, so as to see nothing but the shadows with which she is presently struggling, trying to unravl at a distance of a thousand years, her only clues the faint traces of their passage over this deserted terrain, which is protected from the gulf by seven islands laid out like a shield at the entrance to the bay; a land that reunites Julie and Jack, because he too is exploring it in the depths of his dreams, in the hope of awakening memories of a pre-natal existence. Through his Norman ancestors, come from Norway under the orders of Rölnf-the-Black to conquer a province of France, through all the wielders of the double-bladed axe, a thread connects Jack with Leif the Viking, that ancestor whose bones represent for Julie the numbers 150 to 167 in the excavation reports and whose skull bears the mark of a blow from a metal weapon, leading to the theory that it was his own European companions who murdered him. When they returned to Greenland, did they tell Erik that his son had disappeared? Did Leif's murderers have to wait until the twentieth century to be unmasked? And, if so, who will suffer the vengeance ordained by Erik?

CHAPTER FOUR

I

Jack refused to speak to me on the telephone, making an appointment instead to meet me in a garage in Ville Saint-

Laurent. Once outside the residential neighbourhood west of Laurentian Boulevard, with its restaurants crushed beneath advertising rockets and cones, I pass between rows of brick mausoleums, in which thousands of workers are swallowed up every day of the week. In the lots encircling the factories, stand pieces of dismantled machinery, riddled with rust. I turn a bend in the road and am brought to an abrupt halt behind a long string of vehicles.

The drivers stop blasting their horns when an Army motorcycle with a sidecar speeds past and makes a half-turn in the road opposite me. I park my Mustang and continue on foot. Jeeps bar the route. At either end of the cleared stretch of pavement sits a motorcycle cop, hunched over the handlebars of his Harley-Davidson. Soldiers keep the spectators at a distance. I can see no reason for this sudden deployment of forces.

A series of sharp explosions, and the two motorcycles leap toward each other. A collision seems imminent but, at the last moment, the drivers lift their sidecars from the road and the steel baskets graze each other in passing. A squealing of tires, a wailing of sirens, and the military vehicles and soldiers disappear inside a body shop.

I hesitate for a moment, before entering the shop in my turn. At the top of a metal staircase, behind the glass walls of a gallery that serves as a combination office/dressing-room, the "soldiers" are slipping into mechanics' overalls, laughing and jostling each other. I recognize Denis, the stuntman who works part-time as a projectionist at the Commodore.

Suddenly, I feel the barrel of a revolver pressed against my temple. A plastic hammer snaps against a plastic cylinder, and Jack returns his toy Magnum .307 to its holster. I'm still in the movie house. The show is continuing on an invisible screen. The perspective is reduced to a clever succession of surfaces, disposed in such a way as to keep the viewer constantly off guard. Jack explains that he and his friends have been rehearsing a stunt scene for a war film. We are outside now, in a yard full of vehicles, enclosed by a chain-link fence with a padlocked gate.

"I had the impression I was watching a scene from my own script," I say.

"My brother's partner may have borrowed a few ideas from you for his new film," replies Jack, perched on the wing of a jeep. "But he tells me that his company signed no contract with you."

"I'd have preferred to hear that from Bernard's own lips."

Despite the heat of the sun's rays reflected off the heaps of scrap metal, Jack is still wearing his uniform. The shiny visor of his cap hides his eyes from my view. He is playing with the badge on his tunic. I fear he may have seen me emerging from my search of the Commodore.

"Denis often gives me work as an extra," he says. "Nothing like the role you played in your first film, of course, which I saw recently."

I reply that he must have me confused with someone else, that I've never acted in a film.

"For that, too," says Jack, "I have only your word. It isn't enough to satisfy me. I checked the archives for the names of the victims of the explosion of *The Swan*. Yours is amongst them. Officially, you no longer exist. If I had used a real weapon a few moments ago, I wouldn't have committed a murder, I would simply have brought certain documents up to date."

Behind us, in the shop, the sounds of habitual activity have resumed: the fracas of hammers pounding bodies into shape, the hissing of the pneumatic lift. I know that Jack is lying, that he simply wants to scare me, that my name appears on no list. But I say nothing, waiting for him to play his next card.

"I don't know how you survived that disaster," he goes on. "And, if you stop snooping about, I won't try to find out. I don't like spies, any more than Bernard does. At the Commodore, we form a very tight, united little cell. As for your script, it doesn't interest us."

Before coming to blows with anyone, I always try to prepare myself carefully for the encounter, I never leave things to

chance. I pounce on my adversary only when he believes I'm
a hundred miles away. And I never resist a sudden assault, for
it would very quickly become apparent that I lack the strength
to defend myself. Instead, I feign confusion, simulate help-
lessness, encourage arrogance. Jack smiles as I stammer excuses: since he thinks so little of my script, I'll stop pestering
him. I take a step backwards, deliberately stumble over a tire
iron and topple into a pool of oil. When I pull myself to my
feet, Jack is already unlacing his knee-high boots. He has lost
interest in me. Henceforth, I shall act in the most absolute
secrecy.

II

Following Bernard's departure, Julie suffered another attack
of schizophrenia. She would stop in the middle of corridors,
convinced that a chasm swarming with insects lay open before
her; she would toss lighted matches into wastebaskets; she
would fast for weeks at a stretch. A psychiatrist tried to get her
to talk about her childhood and her dreams, but he didn't
succeed in helping her. Someone gave her LSD and heroin,
and transformed her into a child. She borrowed $400 to pay
for an abortion. After the operation, Jack found her shivering
on a wet mattress: water was dripping from the ceiling, but it
didn't occur to her to move the bed. The landlady screamed
until Jack paid the rent owing on the room. Then he piled
Julie's records, phonograph and dirty laundry in the trunk of
his car. It was snowing: the tires skidded on the icy pavement.

III

I raise the window of the car so the noises from outside will
not drown out my voice on the tape recorder. In front of me,
Jack's Renault stops for a red light. Over a Shell service sta-

tion fly the flags of five different countries. A woman is sun-bathing on the balcony above the entrance to a tavern, her hair in curlers, the ashes from her cigarette dropping onto her gaping dressing-gown. A black man drags a plastic bag full of garbage along the sidewalk. The Renault accelerates when it reaches Boulevard l'Acadie. On my left, a carefully trimmed hedge conceals the fence surrounding Ville Mont-Royal, with occasional openings for pedestrians. People who notice that I'm speaking into a microphone turn quickly away, probably assuming that I'm a member of the police department. The sky is growing dark. I hope there will be enough light to let me take my photos. In the centre of the boulevard, people are waiting to cross to the markets. Jack parks his car at the corner of l'Acadie and Dudemaine. He walks to a flower stall, buys a bouquet of tulips, and strikes up a conversation with a fat, bearded man waiting for the bus.

The empty lot stretches as far as the eye can see, blocks of concrete surmounted by rusty metal rings scattered about it. A teenager is practising his golf strokes. Jack moves toward the abandoned trailer of a tanker truck, tosses his flowers into a mud puddle and returns to his car.

"Today, the Army recovered four top-secret films, which disappeared during a robbery last fall at the International Air-port. The discovery was made by agents, who were led by two anonymous phone calls to a vacant lot at the corner of Rue Dudemaine and Boulevard l'Acadie, in Cartierville."

So as not to let Jack escape me, I am obliged to run a red light. We are now entering the old section of Bordeaux. Large trees cast their shade over the wooden houses. There are stop signs at every corner, forcing the traffic to move at a crawl. Since I'm driving a rented car, a grey Buick, I don't think Jack has recognized me. We've come in sight of the Rivière des Prairies.

"This master-minded theft was kept a secret, possibly be-cause the films detail procedures to be followed by the Depart-ment of Defence in the event of an insurrection. If the thieves had known the true content of the films, they could have sold them for a fortune to foreign spies or other intermediaries."

We are now entering Cartierville. A sign in front of a church announces: BINGO EVERY SUNDAY. An ambulance races toward Hôpital du Sacré-Cœur. Over the entrance to the Pot-au-Feu restaurant hangs a large cooking pot, suspended by ropes from three birch trees. The Renault pulls into the garage next to Jack's house.

"When police retrieved the films, it was discovered that the seals had been broken. If the thieves viewed them, either they failed to comprehend their contents or else they took fright. Investigators from the Ministry of Defence are presently assisting police in making an inventory of the recovered reels. It is still too early to say whether any sequences are missing from the films."

IV

Despite the heat, the man is wearing a brown suit and a felt hat. A high antenna with two lateral bars rises from the trunk of his car. The man climbs the concrete walk on foot. Jack invites him to enter. At this distance and in the absence of any intervening obstacles, the microphone I hid yesterday beneath the coffee-table will transmit their conversation without the slightest interference. By raising the volume of the receiver, I can even go out on the balcony, over which a warm breeze blows, and not miss a word of the interrogation, Jack is giving the man a description of Bernard. Age: 34. Height: five-foot-eleven. Eyes: green. Hair: light brown. Identifying marks: scar on the right palm. Weight: 165 pounds. The curtains of the living-room are drawn, preventing my use of the telescope. But since I am familiar with the arrangement of the furniture in the room, I can easily reconstruct the scene from the sounds I hear. Jack is seated in the leather armchair, fidgeting nervously, while his guest sits calmly on the chesterfield, having expelled the air from a cushion as he lowered himself onto it and placed his feet with a thud on the coffee-table. Only his hand moves as he takes notes with a pencil. To whom does the Commodore belong? he asks in a hoarse voice. To my family, replies Jack. We've had it since the early days of cinema, since the Chaplin era. He goes on to explain that his father left him and his brother very little in the way of hard cash; they had only the receipts from the movie house on which to survive. As a result, they had to give up their studies and go to work. Bernard quickly branched out into film-making, working as a cameraman. He travelled to almost every corner of the world, even Vietnam, sending back reports from spots currently in the news, on behalf of the big American television networks. He returned to Cartierville once or twice a year, at the most. Finally, he accumulated enough capital to launch his own film company. Yes, business was good. He produced a large number of TV documentaries and advertisements. Who would profit from his disappearance? His associates at Focus Films. And, of course, Jack himself, who would then be sole owner of the Commodore.

The sun is beating down on the balcony. I take refuge on the unmade bed of my apartment. Somewhere above me, a couple is quarrelling: doors slam, someone flushes a toilet. I close my eyes and force myself to breathe slowly. The conversation I hear unfolds like an interior monologue, one of those in which you furnish the replies to the questions you have formulated yourself.

"I last saw my brother in the fall. The 15th of October, to be precise. I remember the date because it was the day Belmont Park closed for the season. He spent several hours on the midway with his girl."

In the shooting-galleries, Bernard selected pistols in preference to rifles. He shot blindly, seeming to aim at no point in particular, but with each detonation one of the helium-filled balloons exploded. He won three trophies that evening, a stuffed teddy-bear and two Greek vases, which he gave to Julie for her new apartment. Then they climbed onto the whip, a ride that uses centrifugal force to press its passengers tightly against the railing to which they cling, turning at such a speed that from below their faces merge into a single, undulating line, endowed with a hundred or more mouths opened to laugh or scream. Only then did I emerge from my hiding-place in the crowd, reassured by the confusion created by that ring of revolving bodies, amongst which I tried to distinguish Julie's face. Behind me, I heard the throaty laughter of an enormous plastic woman standing at the entrance to the Chamber of Horrors."

"Did your brother come home that night?"

"No. He slept at his girlfriend's place. I gave you her name and address. In the morning, he left to keep an appointment. Since then, to my knowledge, he hasn't been seen."

"Do you know who he was supposed to meet?"

"A man by the name of Jolin, who apparently had a script to submit to him. The same Jolin—or someone passing for him—approached me the other day in the Commodore, demanding that I pay him for the script. When I refused, he threatened me. Yesterday I caught him tailing me in a car. That man gives me the creeps, he looks and acts like someone who has escaped from an asylum. And he seems to know a great deal about me and Bernard. That's why I decided to call you."

"Did he approach your brother's girlfriend?"

"Not yet. I asked Julie to warn me if he does."

"Do you have a copy of Jolin's script?"

"Yes. Here it is. It reads like the ravings of a madman. There's a lot of violence in it, including a scene involving an attack on a movie house. Even more alarming, the character against whom most of the violence is directed bears an astonishing resemblance to me."

I switch off the receiver. I must tidy up this room. Then I'm going to dive into the pool. I'm not worried about anything Jack might say. In a war, you don't call things by their ordinary names, you use their sacred names. I'm the only one who knows them.

V

I urinate with my eyes closed, relying upon the cold contact of the bowl against my legs to guide the stream. As I close the flap of my shorts, a drop of water strikes me on the brow. I switch on the light and, when my eyes have become accustomed to the glare, I gaze up at the ceiling. There is water under the plaster, forming a yellowish pocket that bursts when I strike it with my fist. At once, the bathroom is flooded, though, thanks to the tiling on the floor and the marble doorsill, the water doesn't spread into the rest of the apartment. I wipe myself off with the bedspread, then dress and proceed to mop up the bathroom. An hour later, sponge in hand, I stand listening to the sound of the air whistling faintly in the gaping hole above me. Cockroaches scurry along the network of pipes filling the space between the two floors. A musty, tomblike odour pervades the room where I lie shivering, my head stuffed beneath a pillow, my right hand gripping the butt of my Lüger. I bite down on the mouth of the barrel, run my tongue over the bead. I wait for some clear emotion to take shape in my mind before squeezing the trigger. Then I replace the weapon in the drawer of my bedside table. I'm no longer cold.

VI

Only death could lend any reality to the existence of someone like Jack, an eternal spectator confined to the same dark little room where nothing ever transpires. No doubt that is why he admires the warriors who attempt through sacrifices to renew the ancient pact with the gods; like Erik the Viking, who causes heads to roll with the blade of his axe. But in a film, whether or not it depends on special effects, when the fatally wounded soldier slumps to the ground, his right arm flinging aside the rifle in an operatic gesture, the bullet always remains invisible because of its great speed.

The cauldron of sentiments cools; the world, whose existence can be ascertained only through its successive paroxysms, becomes blurred; and Jack's memories are dispatched to him in the form of postcards. He will not escape this cabin, not even by identifying with the characters on the screen, becoming, in turn, a secret agent with an electronic arsenal and a bandit at bay in the alleys of Brooklyn. Somewhere, high in the sky, the crew of a B-52 ejects a remote-controlled bomb equipped with a camera, its objective to obtain a plan of the enemy village. The screens have drained the man of his substance; now, they will destroy him. Freedom has taken refuge in the shadows.

The little inspector from the fire-prevention department reeks of alcohol. "My name is Thomas," he says, offering a limp hand that looks as if it had been scarred by chemical aids. "Excuse me for arriving like this unannounced, but we decided to advance the date of our visits this year." Jack asks him to wait a moment, while he gets dressed, then they cross the yard to the Commodore. The inspector points out a fault in the cables holding the fire-prevention lids open; in the event of a fire, they won't snap, as they're supposed to do, their porcelain rings not being positioned directly above the projectors. Thomas prowls about the room, examining a pot of glue, casting a glance at the contents of a trashcan, tapping the walls as if to test their solidity. Finally, he comes upon one of the reels of Erik the Viking. He unrolls a few feet of film, observing that it is made of a nitrate base and therefore highly inflammable; if the reel were jammed for only a few seconds, the heat of the arc lamp would transform it into a torch.

"I never leave the cabin while I'm at work," says Jack.

The visitor nods absent-mindedly and switches on the

blower. Pushing open a vent, he places his hand inside the pipe that rises to the ceiling.

"I don't feel any draught," he says. "It's not functioning."

"I know that, I almost suffocate in here every evening."

The inspector advises Jack to have the repairs completed as soon as possible.

"With those malfunctioning lids and that automatic door, and in the absence of ventilation, this room would empty of oxygen in a matter of minutes and become the equivalent of a blast chamber. Your building wouldn't burn down, it would go up like a stick of dynamite!"

Thomas connects the amplifiers, then strikes a match and passes it over the optic sound recorder, a device that translates into words and music the lighting variations produced by a programmed transparent tape running parallel to the film. Jack can hear the deafening roar produced by the match. As the inspector moves the flickering flame closer to the recorder, the sound resembles the whistling of shells approaching the Commodore.

"Excuse me again," he says. "I'll be back one of these days. I hope you'll have followed my instructions."

Jack escorts his visitor to the door, which he then closes and locks. Then he returns to the candy counter, relishing the familiar odours of the movie house: the dusty curtains, the seats impregnated with grime and sweat, the clandestine cigarettes crushed beneath heels on the aisle floor, an unmistakeable aroma that emanates from every nook and cranny in the house. He can make no distinction between the screen before him and the mirror at the top of the staircase. Everything shifts, slides, undulates, without actually coming into contact, without moving at all, all movement being reduced to imperceptible expansions and contractions within the four walls of the structure.

CHAPTER FIVE

I

Bernard and Julie were not wandering in a physical labyrinth, like that composed of a single street running between two mirrors that reproduced it to infinity; they were lost somewhere deep within a purely verbal maze. It was not the place that escaped them, since without knowing it they had crossed it several times, but the name that identified it and that had been mysteriously effaced. "Armstrong St. no longer exists," the mailman said, fanning himself with his cap. "It's been replaced by Rue Viger—the second street on the left." When a thing no longer has a name, it vanishes, he seemed to think, adhering to the official view, not at all disturbed by the abrupt disappearance of avenues he had covered for twenty years or more, a man who would probably have accepted without comment an administrative decision advising him of his own annihilation. This cryptographic sleight-of-hand propelled the abduction of the minister back to a point in prehistory as distant as the expedition of the Vikings to Sept-Iles, for how could one recognize this bungalow repainted a sky-blue colour, its walls bearing no trace of the explosive charges employed by the police? Children were playing in a sandbox behind the neat little structure, which was the only house on that street whose rear windows commanded a view of airplane hangar number 13. An empty field, spotted with puddles full of tadpoles, stretched all the way to the runway, from which a military transport plane was rising heavily into the air. Even before Bernard was expelled from the house, camera and spotlight in hand, by a furious housekeeper who refused to entertain his request to photograph the interior, Julie knew that nothing had really happened, that the violence was something they'd merely imagined. But perhaps, in the end, they'd find someone real to eliminate?

She stretched her legs awkwardly on either side of the gear

shift and rested her head on Bernard's shoulder. They made their way slowly to the mini-golf course on Boulevard Chambly, where Jack was awaiting them at the sixth hole, aptly named "La Trappe." Struck too hard, the ball ricocheted off the retaining wall and dropped·back into the little valley in the centre of the green felt course. Flies were stalking the players, with their big, multifaceted eyes, buzzing about Jack in such a compact cloud that he was obliged to abandon the game. Placing his putter back on the rack, he complained about the insects to the manager, who was lying on a deck-chair behind the cash, underneath a blue parasol with white tassels. He muttered something about pollution being the cause. Jack looked at him as if he thought he were demented, then invited Julie and his brother to join him for a milkshake in the restaurant next door. Bernard amused himself in passing his straw over the bottom of the waxed carton and noisily sucking up the last drops of milk. Suddenly he announced that he was not going to make a documentary on the abduction of the minister but a feature film about a fictitious revolution. The subject had been suggested to him by a scriptwriter only the week before. Denis and his crew of stuntmen were already busy collecting uniforms, weapons, perhaps even a tank.

In the parking-lot, over which airplanes passed, red maple leaves on their triangular wings, Jack's thoughts were all for his imminent rendezvous with the Commodore's mediumistic screen, foreseeing that death was about to seize the living, that Bernard was about to disappear, that all he would retain of Julie was this photograph taken somewhere on the Côte-Nord, thin traces of snow streaking the bare, grey plateau. No road here linking the isolated houses, no shadow beneath the wan sky. In the foreground, Julie, holding the bridle of a horse, on which sat an Eskimo child. No trace of life that a simple squinting of the eyes would not abolish, transforming the landscape into an abstract canvas composed of three flat horizontal strips.

Jack slips the print back into the transparent envelope in

his wallet and leans toward the window of his projection booth: a dozen spectators at the most are awaiting the beginning of the tale of Erik the Viking. Why does he persist in showing this film, which seems to be of interest to no-one?

II

Julie arrives at her apartment. Her distorted reflection slides over the rust-pitted metal door. A circular table with an oil-cloth cover, a refrigerator, knives hanging from a suspension rack, all these things leap out of the neutral shadows as Jack switches on the two fluorescent bulbs, freezing the kitchen in a sudden tableau: the perforated, soundproof panels on the ceiling, the black and white tiles on the floor, and Julie leaning against Jack, removing her boots.

"Last month," says the young woman, "Saturn entered Gemini, which is my sign. Since then, I've had the firemen here twice, making a shambles of the place to protect me from the smoke and water. And I've had to pay $200 to have the transmission changed in my car."

"And how long is this supposed to last?" asks Jack with a smile.

"Five years, if you're not an initiate. But I calculate closely and with precision: I've got six months to go."

She sets a box of whippets on the table: eighteen round biscuits, arranged in three columns of six, wrapped in embossed paper. She seems irritated by each of Jack's movements: cleaning his teeth with a match-folder, wiping his glasses on his tie, playing with his earlobe, but she says nothing. With her index finger, she crushes the biscuits that Jack washes down with a glass of milk.

"Rat poison," she mutters.

As if partaking in some involuntary Eucharist, Jack finds himself identifying with the biscuits he is consuming. With their thin chocolate coating and their sperm-coloured marsh-

139

mallow filling, they remind him of the testicles that Julie would like to crush with her teeth.

"A biscuit," he says, "can suffer every bit as much as a human being."

"Then I'll tie you and a whippet to a railway track, and when the train passes over we'll see who yells the loudest."

Jack fills a glass with water from the tap, then gargles carefully, irritated by a lump of chocolate that has lodged in a cavity.

"The investigator submitted his report on *The Swan* this morning," he says. "Jolin wasn't on board at the time of the explosion. The producer had decided to shoot some extra footage without the actors."

Julie's only response is to throw the last whippet at his head. Jack pushes her onto the bed and removes her clothing. Later, blowing lightly on her brow, he asks:

"Do you love me?"

"And you?"

Turn in turn, they repeat the question, as they roll over and over on the sheets.

III

The coils of barbed wire whirl more and more quickly above the barracks at the military airport, while the billboards come crashing together. This voyage is not taking place horizontally but vertically, by the simple force of attraction that precipitates me into the school parking-lot, at the end of a spiralling trajectory between restaurants crushed beneath neon signs. The stop is punctuated by the slamming of the car door, then by the scribblings of a pen on paper, but I am no more able to bring myself to a halt than I shall ever be. I must follow the interminable corridors of the school to Julie's classroom, just as I must terminate the sentence, the paragraph, the script. This, despite the agonizing conviction that Julie is escaping me: here, as she stands before the blackboard with its list of examination questions to which the students are responding, their heads bent over their exercise books; here, as her image takes shape imprecisely on the dark screen of memory. Nothing of Julie remains; nothing, moreover, of the universe. Beneath the dazzling projector of my attentive, erotomaniacal, despotic inquiry, all things fade, pale, return to their state of original whiteness, like a sheet of paper, like the sun pouring in the high windows of the classroom and spilling over Julie, over her brown, squinting eyes and her oval face and her breasts clearly outlined by her fluffy sweater. My investigations are preventing me from perceiving the simple, fatal revelation of the appearance lurking behind the reality. I signal to Julie that I'll wait for her outside. Fifteen minutes later, she joins me in the parking-lot, her examination papers tucked beneath one arm.

I introduce myself. She says she was expecting me, that she'd been warned of my visit. She gives me a description of her informer: a man in a brown suit.

"You're looking for Bernard?" she asks, pushing a strand of hair out of her eyes. "I received a letter from him last week: he's making a documentary on IRA attacks in Belfast. He'll be back in Montreal in two or three weeks."

"Did he mention my script?"

"Yes. He calls you his most audacious comrade in anarchy. He believes there should be an element of subversion in everyone's life, that each one of us should conduct a personal terrorist campaign against the social forms of representation. Power is presently exercised by those who control the imaginary. We have exchanged our freedom for a series of fabricated dreams. The great error would be to fight these fictions with truth; they must be opposed with counter-fictions, the collective fable must be unravelled by passing it ever more rapidly between irreconcilably opposite poles."

Julie speaks these words with great application, like someone reciting a text. In fact, she is quoting almost verbatim the opening lines of my script. As for her correspondence with Bernard, it seems to me to be just another fabrication: how could he call me his comrade when he has never even met me? I note that, in my absence, someone has traced his initials on the front fender of my Buick. A gardener is pushing his electric mower in spirals over the lawn. I hate standing out in the open like this. Julie agrees to take me to her place. I follow a complicated route through a new housing development: no-one is tailing me. Most of the residents of the neighbourhood are combatting the dryness with automatic sprinklers, creating a liquid wall through which paperboys dash to leave damp newspapers on doorsteps. Soon, classes will be over. Julie informs me that she plans to return to Sept-Iles, to that wasteland whose barren soil preserves traces of life several thousand years old. Lacking evidence to support it, she refuses to elaborate upon her theory of the axe-wielding massacre of 30-odd Scandinavians, though there is clearly no danger of giving the alarm to the guilty parties. Like me, perhaps, she shrinks from any final solutions, from any resolution of that which is necessarily ambiguous, including her own existence. When the lights are switched on, whether in the theatre or in the mind, the show is over.

Julie lives in an old building near the abandoned tracks of a railway line. An odour of cabbage fills the stairwell, which we climb to the third floor, stepping over sacks of garbage and tricycles on the landings.

In the apartment, Julie leans over the washbasin in the bathroom, splashing her face with water. Then, picking little balls of wool from her sweater, she moves to the kitchen and plugs in the percolator.

"Could you show me the letters?" I ask, wiping the cups that she has washed.

She removes three postcards from her purse. They contain the expected shots of landscapes, with short messages typed on the back. The stamps bear the postmark of Belfast.

"If I wanted people to think Bernard is in Ireland, I'd do

142

exactly the same thing," I say, stirring three spoonfuls of sugar into my coffee. "I'd type those innocuous notes and send them to a friend in Belfast, asking him to mail them back to Montreal. Doesn't it seem strange to you that there is no return address?"

Julie opens one of the examination papers and begins to correct it, telling me that my interest in people corresponds to her own, being confined largely to the traces they leave of their passage through a given place. The absent ones thus become pure creations of our imaginations; in time, come more and more to resemble us. It follows that, in an investigation of this sort, one invariably ends up pursuing oneself. At Sept-Iles, she exhumed the bones of a woman from a mass grave, baptizing her Gudrid, inventing a face, an entire history, for her. And now, in her investigation of the murder of Gudrid, it's the nature of her own death that she is seeking to discover. Of course, she adds, your case is much more dangerous, for Bernard is still alive and may reappear at any moment, bringing you without warning face to face with yourself, with the void.

"If you encountered Bernard," she says, "you would be tempted to make him disappear again."

"Providing I recognized him."

"Don't you even know what he looks like?"

"No. The script was commissioned by mail. I've never seen a picture of him."

She tells me that, in fact, Bernard has never allowed himself to be photographed, that she herself can depend only on memory to conjure up a face that is gradually losing its focus. But then, she adds, anyone at all would be able to introduce himself to me as Bernard, the latter could even approach me under a pseudonym, and I would be none the wiser.

"Why would anyone want to do that?" I ask.

"Why would anyone want to conduct an apocryphal correspondence with me from Belfast? I have no idea. But, in keeping with your theory of a plot, it is essential to consider all angles. Bernard might even be hiding behind the name of someone you've recently met. There's no proof that Jack or Denis is the person he claims to be."

I was expecting some such attempt to sow confusion in my mind, but not from Julie, who, having finished correcting her history papers, reaches out and places her hands over my own, which are clasping the coffee-cup. How is one to retain one's capacity for judgment, when the facts follow one another so rapidly in the tumult of war? Fortunately, in the end, by contradicting one another, they achieve a certain equilibrium in which criticism is self-imposed. If, on the contrary, chance ceased to play a role in these affairs, if each new fact confirmed and augmented its predecessor, I would have no choice but to embark upon a plan of action that would very quickly prove to be absurd. If I suspect Bernard's face to be lurking behind every other, what a temptation to provoke the disappearance in a single blow of all the people who surround me! But I take care not to lose my composure and leave Julie without a word.

CHAPTER SIX

I

Someone is at the door. I make one final check that nothing in the apartment will give me away: the telescope and the radio receiver are in the locker in the basement, the photos are hidden beneath a pile of clothing in the dresser. I can open the door without fear. Leaning against the doorframe, the man in the brown suit blows on the tip of his cigar.

"Monsieur Jolin?" he asks, raising in my direction a pair of eyes that are astonishingly lively, despite the deep shadows that surround them.

I gesture him in. He sinks into an armchair and sets his briefcase on his knees. His crewcut accentuates the squareness of his face, with its two prominent horizontal markings, the eyebrows and the moustache.

"I admire your sense of order," he says. "One wouldn't think your apartment was even inhabited. Indeed, I had a great deal of trouble verifying your existence. Your name appears on no official registers, neither in our dossiers nor in the social-security files. I was beginning to wonder if you hadn't been fabricated in order to set me on the wrong trail. And then you called yesterday to give me your address. Why?"

Hoping to induce him to lower his voice, I reply almost in a whisper:

"I heard you were conducting a search for my friend, Bernard."

His palm held beneath the ash of his Havana cigar, he looks about for an ashtray. I bring him a saucer from the kitchen. During my absence, he lifted the shade of my desklamp and discovered the infra-red bulb.

"Do you develop your own photos?" he asks.

That light must have belonged to a former tenant, I reply, for I spend all my time writing.

"Oh yes, I read your script. Your work bears a close resemblance to my own: things happen, and we want to know what precisely. A crime becomes a story only when I have investigated it. You spend as much time as we do tracking down the guilty parties, but in your case it is to glorify them rather than punish them, that's the only difference."

He opens his briefcase and removes the notebook I gave Jack the other day, along with some file cards covered with notes. He tells me that he is fascinated by the events in my narrative because, despite their extreme improbability, they all lie within the realm of possibility. Like the scene in which the hero eludes his pursuers in a subway tunnel under construction. The description of the setting seemed to him so precise that he concluded it must have been based upon an actual place. A simple verification confirmed, in fact, that I was speaking of the Beauregard Station: the old folks' home above the worksite, the three tunnels intersecting and converg-

145

ing in the marshalling yard, the diamond-shaped mouldings on the concrete walls—nothing ambiguous about any of these details. As for the action itself, the manner in which the protagonist shakes off his enemies in the subterranean labyrinth, drawing them deeper and deeper into the tunnel being blasted out of the rock, then igniting the dynamite, seemed to my visitor more than a little unlikely.

"However," he goes on, leaning toward me, "one of my colleagues reminded me that an identical incident occurred just two weeks ago. There was an explosion in a tunnel under construction, after the worksite was vacated for the night. Beneath the rubble, they discovered a body so mutilated it was impossible to identify it. The victim, probably some teenager looking for kicks, must have accidentally thrown a switch and provoked the explosion. But what I admire most is that your script was written prior to that event."

When my guest unbuttons his jacket, I notice that he has a revolver strapped to his hip, the butt pointing backward, making any attempt to seize the Colt .38 difficult. He takes a photo from his wallet and asks me:

"Is this Bernard?"

I tell him I have no idea. Then he asks me to excuse him for a moment.

While he is in the bathroom, I make a quick examination of the contents of his briefcase: all the documents in it deal with me, my history, my habits. I am convinced that the man in the brown suit is conducting an investigation of me. How otherwise explain his sudden announcement upon his return that he must take his leave? Why doesn't he push the investigation further? Why is he content to question me about a hole in the bathroom ceiling? I treat him with the utmost courtesy, hoping he won't guess that I am aware of his motives. Oh yes, that hole! How dreadful! I've asked several times to have it repaired. No, I don't know what caused it, it was there when I moved in. Once alone, I take the saucer and toss the cigar butt over the balcony railing.

146

II

Julie has very little personal interest in the objects she exhumes, and numbers with a felt pen in order to indicate the position in which they were found. Their co-ordinates are determined by tape-measures attached to stakes and measuring sticks embedded in the walls of the excavation site. Beneath a depth of one foot, the North American soil holds no further treasures, no secrets; archaeologists do not so much dig as scratch. For Julie, the fragments of bone, the arrowheads, the scraps of metal, represent the interchangeable words of that history that she must unravel in the interest of scientific exactitude, a process that excludes all links, however tenuous, however invisible, between the events that occurred about 1000 AD in a Greenland colony and the vacation spent with Bernard on the same strip of sand connecting the sea and the tundra. The Viking settlement certainly bore little resemblance to the Commodore, judging from the stone foundation and peat walls of Julie's scale model of the former. No resemblance either between Bernard and Thorvald, the leader of the Greenland expedition. So why does she persist in seeing her own fate as being mysteriously tied in with these labelled bones displayed in a glass case in an archaeological laboratory?

III

The slapping of the waves, the sea air, the gulls hanging above the barges, and Julie armed with a Lüger, standing atop a heap of rocks laid bare by the outgoing tide, emptying the magazine of her pistol. Wrapped about the steel butt, her hands leapt with each detonation, but the recoil did not cause her stiffened arms to bend. Her eyes didn't even blink when the bullet, ricocheting off a rock, followed an unpredictable trajectory. She hoped simply that death would not leave a look of surprise on her face. In the car parked on the sandy shoulder of the road, Bernard lowered the sun visor to protect his eyes from the glare of the sunlight on water. Repressing a desire to break into wild laughter, Julie returned to the road, one foot dragging slightly, for the strap of her sandal had snapped. She slid into the front seat of the car, exclaiming as her thighs came in contact with the burning leather upholstery. Bernard drew the weapon from the belt of her skirt, where she had slipped it, and returned it to the glove compartment. The Pontiac left the coast and disappeared into a forest of giant firs, leaving behind it a long trail of dust.

Several minutes later, it drew to a halt before the bungalow that Bernard had rented for the duration of the filming. The documentary on the archaeological excavations having been completed, the technical crew was already on its way back to Montreal. Bernard planned to spend the night alone with Julie. He waved to a neighbour, who was seeding his lawn.

"It's a waste of time, I know," said the big man, scratching his hairy chest. "The grass doesn't grow. It's that sand that the wind keeps blowing in."

He gestured toward the farther side of the road, where the tundra began. The empty, rectilinear horizon resembled that of the sea. But, on this side of the road, you could hear the incessant hum of television sets and electric lawnmowers, and the houses, all identical, stood pressed as tightly together as they did in Cartierville. The only harsh note was sounded by the totem pole a Montagnais family had sculpted from an old telephone pole, the beaks, muzzles and claws of its sacred beasts all facing northward. Bernard stood motionless for a moment on the doorstep, an absent look on his face, then, instead of entering the house, he moved slowly away from it, his right hand gripping Julie's wrist. He crossed the narrow street and the cracked sidewalk, then his shoes sank into the peat-moss. The surface was perfectly flat, but he had the strange impression that he was climbing a steep slope. As far ahead as he could see, as far as his strength might carry him, there was nothing. He stopped and gazed at Julie.

148

"Shall we keep going?"

"The strap on my sandal is broken. And, out there, you can't walk in a straight line. With no point of reference, you just end up going in circles."

On this vast stage, with no props and no sets, Bernard knew they would soon have nothing to say to each other, they would forget their lines, nothing they did would ever bring an end to the play. So they returned to the bungalow, to the kitchen where Julie removed two steaks from the refrigerator while he uncapped a bottle of beer. The radio was blaring. If you take a bee from its hive, thought Bernard, if you place it in complete solitude, it will die in a matter of hours. If ever again he attempted to leave the hive, he would take no-one with him. But what difference would that make? He existed for Julie only when he was absent. Likewise, he would disappear only if he remained resolutely at her side. Each time that she stood waiting for him, watching the corner of the street where he would step off the bus, each time that she awoke with a start because he was no longer holding her, was he not as close to her as he would ever be? The world was always several steps behind him. No-one, not even Julie, could prevent him from taking flight, from returning to the tundra whose sparkling line stretched straight across the kitchen windows. Perhaps he would end up going in circles; but the one he encountered when he returned to the point of departure, he would kill without a moment's hesitation. Bernard had no friends, he was looking for someone he could challenge to a duel.

IV

Trucks filed by, one after the other. During an interval of silence in the hubbub of diesel engines, Bernard could hear Julie's footsteps as she followed behind him with the portable tape recorder. Trying to make out the sign of a restaurant, he stopped in the middle of the temporarily deserted road. In the distance, the spaces between the dashes in the dotted line became shorter and shorter, until it resembled a continuous ribbon.

V

Bernard had returned from two months of filming in Sept-Iles. Jack had imagined this reunion too often not to be disappointed by the actual event: the windows of the house lit up, a Buick parked in the driveway. His brother was sleeping, fully dressed, a bottle of saki on his chest. He was nothing but a combination of bronzed skin, red and grey hair, blue denim: an exhausted character who didn't complete his sentences, had trouble rolling his cigarettes (there were shreds of tobacco even in the sugar bowl) and spent an eternity in the bathroom, from which periodically there emerged a number of irritating sighs, accompanied by the rustling of the newspaper brought back from the pharmacy with a bottle of laxative. Bernard took frequent walks in the streets of Cartierville, hoping chance might throw him into the company of old acquaintances, but he met no-one; the neighbourhood had undergone a great many changes. As for Jack, he spent his time hounding loan companies, not one of which would give him another mortgage on the movie house, which was already mortgaged to the hilt. He had just returned from one of these exhausting excursions when Bernard introduced him to Julie.

VI

Jack opened the door. The cat took advantage of the opportunity to dash between Bernard's legs. Impossible to retrieve it in all that snow. While Bernard unfastened his boots, Jack set up the chessboard in the kitchen. Then he held out his closed fists.

"Left," said his brother and inherited the black men.

Bernard had made a bet that he could drink four glasses of gin in quick succession and still win the game. Ten minutes later, dead drunk, he upset the board and advanced upon Jack, who backed laughing onto the porch. Bernard lost his balance and toppled over the railing into the snow-filled yard, which, with the neighbouring houses and yards, all identical, all geometrically disposed, formed one of the black and white squares of a giant chessboard, on which the falling snowflakes slowly covered Bernard up.

CHAPTER SEVEN

I

My script: last salvo of a volley of gunfire, spitting out its shells in accordance with a temporal parabola of increasing length, the origins of which lie in the lost years of my adolescence, when I concocted flame-throwers from insecticide spray-cans filled with gasoline: soldering closed the end of a pipe, drilling a hole in the metal, inserting a wick, filling the improvised cannon with the black powder from firecrackers purchased in novelty stores; then, with my improvised arsenal, trying to blow up the commuter train running between Montreal and Cartierville. I had stolen some nitric acid, sulphuric acid and glycerine from the school laboratory and, seated that morning on the wet grass, I emptied the three flasks into a Seven-Up bottle, hoping thus to produce nitroglycerine. The sun was causing the grass to steam and burned hot on my face. I held the preparation between my knees, watching it darken and begin to bubble, threatening at any moment to spill over onto my hands. At the last moment, I hurled the bottle across the lawn, where it exploded. A red vapour rose into the air, assuming the form of a giant mushroom, then was slowly dispersed by the wind. There was an overpowering odour of rat-ten eggs. This time I had come very close to realizing my goal, nitroglycerine explodes only at 65° F and it was not yet that warm. Now, however, I am approaching my objective: I have arranged the lines of my script like columns of infantry; beneath each sequence, I have planted mines. All that I'm lacking is a director. The means that Bernard will use to execute my plans will not stop at the cinematic.

And now that I have given myself up to this interior polylogue (not a monologue because composed of too many strange voices, which channel through mine the product of their harmony or discord), now that I am playing this diatonic piece for pen, the dominant phrases come to me from Bernard, as if all the words I attribute to him had fused with my thoughts, revealing themselves more clearly in Bernard's silence and absence than in his improbable presence, so that when I try to imagine what he would say to me if he were seated here in this armchair before me, I hear only a dull, steady murmur, like those debates one sometimes conducts with oneself. I approach the window and watch Jack changing the signs: a new show will begin tonight. As usual, I shall slip into the place after the cash has closed, so as not to be spotted.

II

The condemnation drawn up according to the binary system runs up against the valiance of our soldiers, who mutiny and invade the city. The final combat is unfolding here in this quarter, which has been ravaged by bombing raids. Behind those broken windows, a bazooka fires upon one of the armoured cars climbing the street: two men emerge from the flaming wreck and roll on the ground. The enemy finally has a face, upon which I draw a bead with my telescopic sights. The terrain is small but it is ours. And no archaeologist will need to probe the debris: no more searching for some nonexistent past. It will be obliterated, not with words or images but with gunpowder—if need be, with a million tons of TNT.

Suddenly the guns fall silent, and I hear Bernard's voice, quiet but audible in the silence of the uninhabited city, about which are scattered signs bearing the words: ABC DEMOLI-TION COMPANY. And I observe the jeering smile of my future director as he asks me if an armoured car could actually pass through this block of houses or if the walls shouldn't be made of pasteboard. He adds that Denis and his crew of stunt-men will be wearing fireproof asbestos underwear, over which their uniforms will burst into flame, producing a startling effect. Small charges of nitro will be buried about the site to simulate the explosion of shells.

III

Because the film is old, it looks as if it were raining on the wide avenue, where motorists have abandoned their cars and raced for shelter from the bombs that a massive aerial armada is about to drop on the city. The earth begins to tremble, causing the camera, as well as the seat from which Jack observes the proceedings, to shake. Now he is on his feet, moving quickly up the centre aisle of the empty Commodore, realizing that he must waste no time in taking refuge underground. Because the main door is blocked, he moves to the emergency exit. It swings open abrutply, like a trap-door, and he looks down a hundred feet to the sidewalk, where a few corpses lie strewn about, the victims of the first explosions. He just avoids falling by clinging to the doorframe. Struggling desperately, he man-ages to close the swinging door, which hangs heavily on its strap hinges. That the movie house is currently suspended high in the air, its façade turned toward the ground, Jack is obliged to admit, but he cannot understand why he is still walking on the floor and not on the wall. Glancing at the clock next to the candy counter, he finally understands: the numbers are inverted, the twelve on the bottom, the six on the top. This temporal distortion has caused a rupture in space, and Jack will be able to leave the movie house and rejoin the real world only at the end of a long,and fatal fall.

IV

Night. Headlights illuminate a mountain of empty oil drums. The car makes a half-turn and comes to a stop behind a metal shed. The motor continues to idle. Bernard slams the door, opens the trunk, removes a shovel and begins to dig. Then he opens a canvas sack and takes a machine-gun from it. Resting the barrel of the weapon on a drum, he takes aim at a tank in the neighbouring refinery and fires. There is an explosion. A column of flames lights up the sky, against which Bernard can be seen wrapping up his rifle and climbing back into the car.

V

The one who narrated the sagas, on the long winter evenings, was under the obligation to keep his audience from falling asleep, under pain of losing his honour and seeing himself thrown out into the cold, which would have sealed his lips forever.

VI

Jack is previewing a new film. Large flags flap feebly in the thick fog, through whose grisaille the buildings are barely discernible. The pavement echoes hollowly beneath the feet of passersby, underground shelters having been built beneath them. Here, the insurgents are dying, following a clandestine uprising. An intolerable sadness seizes Jack. Leaning on the back of the seat in front of him, he watches as two enemy patrols pass each other on the screen in a fracas of hobnailed boots, then whirl about to exterminate each other with bursts of machine-gun fire. The scene slowly dissolves.

CHAPTER EIGHT

I

Someone must have noticed Bernard when he left the vacant lot near the refinery. The flames that mounted from the reserve tanks lit up his car as brightly as daylight; it would even have been possible to note the numbers on his licence plate. Almost at once, he spots the enemy patrol following him on the boulevard, which at this late hour is almost deserted. He heads toward the predetermined spot for eluding any eventual adversaries and regaining the occupied zone. On the sunken expressway, he half-expects each viaduct he passes beneath to explode, but the only disturbance is a momentary burst of static on the car radio; and, in the rearview mirror, the road behind him is not transformed into an impassable demarcation line. The cars continue to criss-cross above, sheet metal orbiting about concrete, and nothing announces the approach of the critical mass; on the contrary, energy decreases as in the heart of a cooling gas. Soon, Bernard's jeep and the pillars of this viaduct will intersect like two incorporeal images; soon, all will be nothing but icy light.

He has enough of a lead on them to park the vehicle behind the old folks' home and crawl beneath the wire fence into the subway construction site; but the lights of his adversaries' car pick him out as he descends the steep slope leading to the unfinished tunnels. The strap of the machine-gun cuts into his right shoulder, and his rubber boots sink into the mud, coming away with loud sucking sounds that betray his position. He enters the workers' shed, using the key he borrowed the day before. From a rack, he takes a spool of electric wire. A face is watching him: the eyes, two nails surrounded by a coat-hanger twisted to resemble the frames of a pair of glasses; the mouth, a rough outline drawn on the plywood wall; the nose, a triangular piece of wood.

He leaves by the opposite door. Since the cabin occupies the entire width of the tunnel, his pursuers will have to force the door, leaving him a few moments of respite. He follows a footbridge of thick planks set a few feet above the ground. His gun swings from his shoulder, at times striking one of the hundreds of metal supports that prevent the ceiling from collapsing. Behind him, he hears a shot. The bullet ricochets off the wall with a whining sound. Impossible to shoot with any precision in these shadows, broken at infrequent intervals by garlands of naked bulbs; impossible to take aim at anything moving amongst this mass of machinery and scaffolding. He descends a ladder and zigzags across a section of the site open to the sky, then stops to catch his breath in the shelter of a cement mixer, gazing at the three tunnels that sink into the rock ahead of him. He knows that a mile farther on they merge, where the construction crew is preparing to break through to the marshalling yard and to link up with another crew coming in the opposite direction. He takes the centre tunnel, hoping the thick mud will induce his pursuers to choose one of the other two, which, with their dry cement walls, are more accessible than the one he is in but considerably longer. And, indeed, when he reaches the juncture, after an exhausting run, the sound of voices reaching him from behind the left gallery verifies his calculations. He has time to attach the wire to the detonator and return with it to a bend in the tunnel, where he takes cover. Wielding pistols, two soldiers suddenly come into view. They pass him and move on down the tunnel. With a coin, Bernard tightens the screws on the copper conductors leading to the dynamite charge. Then he presses the detonator. One of the two men emerges coughing from a cloud of dust; he must have been walking behind his companion. Bernard sets his rifle on automatic fire and squeezes the trigger. Lifted from the ground by the impact of the explosion, the man's body dances for a moment in the air, then topples backward. Bernard dips his handkerchief in the trickle of water at his feet and knots it over his mouth. No-one heard the explosion on the surface. It is a matter now of following the designated route, to emerge by way of a ventilation shaft in the open air of the occupied zone.

II

The enemy has infiltrated the tunnels of the subway, severing the last connection between the occupied zone and the outside world and thus preventing any further commando operations of the type carried out by Bernard against the refinery. The clearing offensive has failed. But they still hold the head of D—— Bridge. Severe restrictions have been imposed regarding food supplies, wood, munitions, fuel. Bernard commands a battalion charged with defending City Hall. Not a single windowpane is left intact, but sheets of heavy cellophane found in the basement have been stretched over the frames to prevent the snow from blowing off the frozen river from reaching the interior, where the men sit warming themselves about fires fuelled by the office furniture. The enemy has not yet succeeded in crossing the river, but is content to bombard the zone from batteries set up on the farther shore. On the north front, however, it is gaining a little more territory each day. A reconnaissance aircraft flew over the encircled troops but, in obedience to the order to save munitions, it was not fired upon.

III

Orders: since the enemy is arming itself with mirrors, walk

behind your shadow; in this way, you will not be blinded. Shoot without hesitation at your own reflection. Victory will belong to those who master the correlation between shadow and light.

The warriors will begin by blowing up the radio and television towers and the presses of the major newspapers. In the absence of news reports, the civilians will not dare to venture into the streets, but will remain locked up in their homes, peeking from behind their window blinds. They will see us file past, bayonets attached to our rifles, leading women in chains behind our vehicles, the treads of which will chew up the pavement. The file-past will last for hours, following a circular route, provided that numbers remain sufficient.

The warriors exist only outside themselves. They will die rather than retreat into memory and thought. The orders will not come from above or below, they will come from nowhere. Every command will be considered a diversionary tactic, and will be treated as such.

Your spies will be everywhere. The enemy will also have his. If you should unmask one, take care not to kill him; he will be more valuable to you alive than dead. Weighing your words and actions carefully, you will impart false information to the enemy spies.

Burn, smash all the screens. Reverse the logic of the representation.

IV

An enemy climbed to the lieutenant's tent and tossed a grenade inside it. When he attempted to escape in the direction of the river, Bernard seized his rifle: an M-16. The recoil almost dislocated his shoulder, but the enemy didn't get back to his feet. Very simple: a detonation in the right ear and, at the same time, a silhouette crumpling in the distance.

V

Hundreds of men have left their fingerprints on the rectangles of blue-and-pink plaster: sole traces of their existence now that the demolished houses are nothing but a fine dust floating in the atmosphere; now that the demolitioners' cranes have left, intact—where once there were walls and floors—only a single partition, its multicoloured patterns exposed in places to reveal the bare brick. Jack and Julie walk through the field of rubble, amongst ruins that offer a natural setting for a war film and that will probably be cleared away by bulldozers within a few days. Here, in an apartment smelling of incense, Julie once sat, her legs crossed, facing a bare white wall. Behind her, the master paced the room, which was as cold as an icebox, its windows open to the January snow, contemplating his glassy-eyed disciples, attentive to the slightest relaxation of their bow-taut spines, to the slightest muscular retraction that would betray the passage of a thought or an emotion. To float in space, to shatter without a sound, to sink into the original divine oneness! When the whirlwind passed, the master's rod struck Julie without inflicting any pain. Only the images dissolved. Now she searches for fragments of that wall, turning over boards with her foot.

Dressed in his eternal brown suit, the investigator advances with a heavy step, stopping now and then to pick his way through the debris.

"The area is infested with rats," he says to Jack, tearing the band from a big cigar with his thumb.

"It was Julie who suggested this spot to me, when you refused to meet me at my place."

"There was a good reason for that. Jolin has hidden microphones in your house. And he has a telescope on the balcony of his apartment, through which he can observe all that goes in the neighbourhood. I would bet he can even get a close-up of the pimple on your nose."

He spits out a few shreds of tobacco, then, eyeing Julie

seated on a beam, asks:

"Do you close the curtains of your bedroom at night?"

An airplane is moving back and forth across the sky, towing an advertising banner behind it, but it doesn't approach closely enough to allow Jack to decipher the message.

"How did you find out...?" he asks.

"The other day, in your living-room, I noticed a microphone similar to the ones we use. I waited until Jolin was out to pay him a visit, and I discovered his little spying arsenal."

"And he did all that simply to find my brother? Because he suspects us of hiding the truth?"

Spreading his legs, the big man pulls his pants away from his rump. A thread of perspiration runs between his eyebrows and disappears behind his sunglasses.

"He's not trying to find anyone, he's up to something. Have you read his script?"

"Not really, no. What's it all about?"

"Isolated acts of violence, leading little by little to all-out warfare between a group of insurgents and the army. In a word, utter chaos. Probably only the opening scene would interest you. It takes place inside a movie house in the suburbs. Blood is flowing across the screen. The spectators all seem hypnotized. The narrator explains that they are contemplating the captive forms of their own anger. They emerge and disperse in the streets. At that very moment, the movie house blows sky high. And do you know what film was showing in that cinema? Erik the Viking."

"I didn't hire you to fabricate plots for me," retorts Jack angrily. "I know how you people play upon the naïveté of your clients, hoping to frighten them into paying for further investigation of imaginary plots. I have no interest in anything Jolin might write. But your ravings are costing me $75 a day, plus costs. And since you haven't brought me even the smallest scrap of information about my brother, you may consider your contract terminated."

The big man shrugs wearily.

"I was planning to quit the case anyway. Police methods are of no use in solving this mystery. But check for yourself, you'll find a microphone under your coffee-table."

"The one you put there yourself," replies Jack, turning on his heel and moving toward his car.

"Did you make up that story?" asks Julie.

"Me or someone else: what does it matter?"

The airplane passes slowly above them, its message in tow. Instead of raising her head, Julie lowers her gaze and watches the shadow of the banner as it passes over the rough terrain. At this moment, the city seems as empty and deserted to her as the tundra north of Sept-Iles, where all progression invariably brings one back to the point of departure. Jack blows the horn. She gestures to him to go on without her.

"In some strange way, that fellow is profiting from the absence of his brother," says the investigator. "He now finds himself the sole owner of the movie house and . . . Why do you sleep with him? It's as plain as day you can't stand him."

Waving goodbye, the investigator moves down the sidewalk. Julie remains alone. She is used to this. Even during archaeological expeditions, the comrades with whom she shares a tent for months at a time seem more remote to her than the hypothetical creatures whose bony, quasi-mineral remains she exhumes before placing them in shoeboxes. This is why she is so fascinated by Bernard, whom she sees as being reduced already to the minute traces he has left of his passage. Not that she thinks of him as dead, bereft of all vitality, but rather as having disappeared and being capable, therefore, of making his appearance suddenly felt in places other than those connected with everyday life. Like those inhabitants of Greenland, with their large, flourishing cities, trading in furs and walrus tusks, who in the space of a mere century became extinct, their deserted dwellings showing traces neither of invasion nor of natural disaster. But how can an entire people perish like that, without even a struggle, leaving no record of itself nor of the vast continent it had discovered? And what was it that Bernard had pitted himself against, engaging in a combat that united him with warriors who had lived a thousand years before and who were now buried near Sept-Iles—what, if not the very oblivion into which his brothers were sinking? He who falls still clinging to his weapons, his courage not yet having failed him, will never know peace; he will return, again and again, in a thousand different guises, until the final confrontation between the gods and the void. Then, when the last star is extinguished, there will remain only the night to light up the sky. Impossible, meanwhile, to capitulate to the point of becoming one of those characters towering over a crowd of spectators in a darkened hall, uttering lies, persuading their listeners with each word spoken that the final word has been said. Dummies and trick shots, thinks Julie, that's all there is between the credits and the words THE END. Far more preferable is the film that displays no logic and no order, that incorporates all the possible itineraries: an incompleteness that only the violence and the explosion on board *The Swan* rendered possible by interrupting the fossilizing mechanism of creation. So that there are no more actors, no more film-makers, only men at the moment of disappearance, struggling in a common crepuscular zone, their only makeup the features that death will imprint on their faces. And under the effect of that constantly deferred sentence, that off-stage destiny simultaneously identifying and exposing each of the minor dramatic effects, the actors of *The Swan*—not those whose corpses lie in a common grave but the luminous beings who vibrate 24 times a second on the Commodore's screen—take their place beside Bernard and the Vikings of Greenland, in that region where the make-believe packs charges of energy far more intense than those of reality: an imbalance that occasionally results in short-circuits. And Julie, like Jolin perhaps, finds herself at one of those breaking-points, her consciousness oscillating dangerously between poles that are separated by centuries of history. Let this vacillation intensify, accelerate, and she will pass through to the other side of this landscape of

162

grey houses encircling a field of rubble.

CHAPTER NINE

I

Jack is recovering from hay fever, complicated by laryngitis. His sickness excuses him from any serious business. He spends his time reading third-rate spy novels and news tabloids, and sprawled in front of the television set. He stupefies himself with medication. Nothing upsets him or troubles him, not even the financial state of his business. Later, the first sign of recovery: he is able to smoke again.

II

I'm suffering from a loss of being. How describe this absence? Let me put it this way: I get up with the intention of continuing my investigation, of interrogating Julie again, and almost at once I am prostrated by fatigue, my legs falter, for the first time I become aware of their existence. The phenomenon is repeated in my head: it begins to ache, I realize that I have one. Otherwise, nothing. Outside these physical complaints, nothing at all. A total absence of feelings and thoughts. And when I encounter someone on the street, I am struck by the fear that he may suddenly and inexplicably attack me. All my efforts are devoted to finding a solution to this enigma. Meanwhile, I am content to sit on the balcony and gaze at the Commodore, or listen to the conversations picked up by the microphones I've planted all over the place. It's as if some external force had taken control of my energies and confused my thoughts. But I haven't thrown in the towel, I'm waiting for whatever it is that is insidiously attacking me to reveal itself. For the moment, I can almost believe that I'm watching

163

a show. But one false step, and I'll be right in the thick of the action. The space about me is filled with whizzing bullets. They announce their presence with that brief, high whistle that grazes the ear and the soul. Here, reason operates on a different level, takes a form other than that of speculation. Danger belongs to the realm of fiction.

III

Eight Goths and 22 Norwegians, on a voyage of exploration west of Vineland. We camped near two rocky isles, a day's journey north of that rock. The next day, we went fishing. On our return, we found ten men slaughtered. Ave Maria, deliver us from evil. There are ten men on the shore, guarding our vessel, fourteen days voyage from that isle. Year 962.

IV

Jack awakens. He has all the time in the world. He gazes at his watch, telling himself that if he never takes his eyes off it, the hours will cease to pass; that if he takes stock of all the gradations of light when the sun rises, he will no longer be able to differentiate the day from the night. In this way, he will dissolve into the oneness of death, disintegrate with the ashes of his last cigarette. He no longer believes in life, only in its antithesis, that void that is applied to words and gestures like silvering to a mirror.

CHAPTER TEN

I

The backfire of motorcycles, periodically drowning out the

ticking of the clock on the mantelpiece: that's about all my receiver has recorded for the past two hours. Suddenly, the front door slams. I apply my eye to the telescope, which is already aimed at the living-room: I see Jack walking upside-down, the result of the customary inversion of objects when viewed through a telescopic lens. He stands for a moment before the window, his myopic eyes raised in my direction, then reaches out and snaps the curtains shut. Suddenly, I hear tearing sounds: he's removing the adhesive tape holding the microphone to the underside of the coffee-table. How long has he known that I've been spying on him? How long has he been leading me on? Did all those discussions I recorded merely constitute a series of lengthy dialogues designed to mislead me? Now I hear the sounds of heavy breathing, ampli-fed by the speaker.

There is a crash, followed by a steady, high-pitched hum. Jack has just destroyed my microphone.

II

For the past few days, Jack has been attempting through language to attain the neutralization of his being; and now he believes himself to be on the right track, for the words come to nothing, they return upon themselves, following a circuitous trajectory that must be constantly accelerated, for no matter how beautiful or truthful the phrases, the only thing that matters is the instantaneousness of their disappearance, the magnificent void they leave in their wake. A page becomes blank only when it has been written on.

III

In Greenland, the ground has thawed for the last time. The corpses Julie unearths this summer, five centuries after their deaths, still wear brightly coloured garments. And the cloaks worn in the Grand Duchy of Bourgogne, in the fifteenth century, come into fashion again.

IV

War alone will allow us to exist. The gestures, words and texts promoting acts of violence: all state-approved.

V

When the plane sets down at Sept-Iles, Julie rents a room in an isolated motel with an artificial stone façade, adjacent to a restaurant. Without a word, the owner pockets the rent money and hands over the key. Julie stretches out on a deck-chair and watches the cars passing on the road that skirts the sea-shore. On adjoining lots, bungalows and billboards sit among weeds.

Julie crosses the parking-lot, passes through the empty dining-room and finds the owner behind the swinging doors of the kitchen. Bare to the waist, he is in the act of pulling the plug from the sink. Beans and chunks of meat bubble to the sur-face, the pipes vibrate, and suddenly the water is sucked away. The little man says that none of the other members of the archaeological society have arrived yet. Julie gets into her rented car and heads for the eastern shore. When she reaches the old excavation site, she stops. The grounds surrounding the hot-dog stand have been covered with asphalt. She orders a cold chicken sandwich with mayonnaise.

Julie belongs to a world devoid of tragedy; one which, with its four continents, suddenly seems smaller than the black sur-face of this 1000-square-foot parking-lot. She sits at a picnic-table, hidden from the eyes of the other customers by a large parasol. If she remains as still as a statue, she may eventually be transformed into stone; then, making contact with the memory of the earth, she will see the faces of the gods.

She rises and moves toward the sea. A child is digging holes in the sand at regular intervals and planting sticks in them, to form a large rectangle. Then he lays strips of bark over the tops of his miniscule columns. He's building a temple. The tide is rising, the waves are coming closer and closer. To retard their advance, the little boy digs a trench, then runs in search of a board to serve as a roof for his structure. He is clearly enjoying this mad race against the sea, which has time on its side. But eternity plays no role in this little game that is being played out before her. His fingernails black with earth, his hair wet from the sea spray, the child stands with a strange smile on his face as the ocean rolls over the ruins of his unfinished temple.

CHAPTER ELEVEN

I

A sliding ladder leans against the side of the split-level bungalow. Denis is seated on the roof, his legs dangling over the edge, chewing a wad of gum. He takes a deep breath, clicks his heels together and jumps. For a moment, his body looks gigantic against the backdrop of the sky. Then he hits the grass, bounces once and rolls into a row of shrubs.

"No good," he says, getting to his feet. "I was reaching for the ground with my feet, instead of waiting for it to come up to me."

The soles of his shoes have left inch-deep prints in the soil.

"Would you like to come and work for me as a stuntman?" I ask him.

He looks at me for a moment, his gaze absent, then blinks his eyes several times.

"Excuse me," he says. "Whenever I jump, my brain strikes

the wall of my skull and leaves me stunned for a while."

"Do you have any dynamite?"

"No, but I can lay my hands on some. Why?"

I tell him that filming will begin on my script tomorrow evening, that the opening scene involves the explosion of a movie house in the suburbs.

"Who's producing the film? Bernard? You found him, then?"

"Obviously. But he's changed so much you won't recognize him."

He accepts my offer and I fill him in on the details. There is a glow in his crafty little eyes. He persists in looking upon me as a fool, whom he can manipulate at will. I have no time to show him that this is not the case. Explanations carry war further from the absolute, bring it closer to pure chance; then it becomes a game. And my combative forces have already suffered a serious setback from the very duration of the campaign. No question of slowing down now. I know Denis will carry out my orders, as aberrant as they seem, if only to lay his hands on the money I've offered him. He promises to keep my plans a secret, and giving him a substantial cash advance, I take my leave. A short distance from the house, I stop at a service station to fill up on gas. A bell rings in the attendant's office, with the sound of a coin dropping into a machine. Without the invisible combats that keep things moving, without the primordial chaos that subsists beneath the semblance of order, the sun would emit darkness and the truth would be error incarnate. I didn't allow Jack to edit the film shot on board *The Swan*, any more than I will let him concoct a tale by means of which he would restore peace.

II

Because of the cold and the lack of food, some men go mad. They return to the savage state, hiding in holes. At night, when they emerge to go in search of something to eat, flames illuminate the no-man's-land and they are mowed down by gunfire coming from both camps. Bernard's men are still holding City Hall, but the enemy has succeeded in crossing the river. Communications inside the occupied zone are becoming more and more difficult. Despatch riders carrying messages run the risk of falling upon enemy patrols. There is no way Bernard can determine the authenticity of the orders received, since the enemy seems to have broken the codes. All the same, he has succeeded in clearing the entire length of a street, using a flame-thrower and working through the sewers. And morale has improved since he managed to provide his combatants with hot water, heated in a barrel on a stove. For Bernard, time is no longer calculated by the number of days that have passed but by the number of dead and wounded; a progression which, in the absence of reinforcements, is irreversibly reaching its termination. The number of cases of hallucination resulting from hunger has dramatically increased: the men see tanks and cannons where, in fact, there are none. There are moments when even Bernard cannot prevent himself from wondering if the entire war is not an illusion. Did he really see that emaciated corporal gnawing a large bone torn from the carcass of a horse or a man, or did he merely imagine it? One thing remains certain: death.

III

The dead man's boat was lifted from the water and placed between four posts, at the centre of a circle of large wooden statues carved to represent humans. Off to one side lay Erik the Viking, in his wooden coffin. A bench was installed in the boat and covered with padded cushions of Greek silk brocade and a pillow made of the same material. The body was dressed: culottes, stockings, boots, a coat and a caftan of gold brocade adorned with marten pelts. Then it was placed in a seated position in the boat, resting on the padded cushions. Intoxicating beverages were placed nearby. When this was done, the men seized a dog, cut it in two and tossed the two halves on board. They placed Erik's weapons at his side, brought two horses dripping with sweat, dismembered them with blows of a sword and placed the meat in the boat.

The wives of the dead man were asked:

"Who wishes to die with him?"

One of them replied:

"Me."

Two other women were charged with guarding her and accompanying her everywhere. She spent the following days drinking and singing and seemed quite gay and content. When it came time for the funeral, the men passed in single file before her. Then they carried her to the top of a frame-like trestle and raised her three times in the air, while she exclaimed: "Look, my father and mother!" And: "Look, all my dead relatives seated together!" And a third time: "Look, my dead lord in the kingdom beyond! It's so lovely and green! Warriors and servants are gathered about him! And he's calling me! Let me go to him!"

Jack notes the bright circles at the top of the screen, warning him that he must set the second projector in motion. For a few moments, as it unwinds, the film is opaque, then, when the new circles appear, he flips a switch to stop the first projector and the second one takes over.

They escorted her to the boat, where she removed her two bracelets and gave them to the woman called the Angel of Death, who was assigned to be her executioner. Then, one by one, they entered the tent and had intercourse with her. When they had finished, they laid her beside her lord. Two men seized her feet; two others, her hands; while the old woman called the Angel of Death slipped a lace about her neck, passing the ends to two men who held them tight. Then she approached with a long, broad knife, sank the blade between the woman's ribs then removed it. The two men held onto the

170

lace until they were sure the woman was dead. At that moment, Leif, the son of Erik, appeared on the scene. He seized a burning brand and approached the boat. Soon, the whole vessel was aflame: the tent, the deck, the hull. A large mound of earth was erected above the ashes, at the spot where the boat had been lifted from the water, and a beech post was planted in the centre of it, bearing the name of the dead man. Then the mourners went on their way.

IV

At this moment, the film breaks. Swearing, Jack switches off the projector, while the spectators in the hall applaud derisively. He looks in vain for the pot of glue, consoling himself with the knowledge that he is showing this old film for the last time. Tomorrow, a double feature will be on the bill, a program that will draw all the dirty old men in the neighbourhood.

V

Cartierville. Worm-eaten boats with crumbling hulls, locomotives rusting on side-rails, abandoned cars in an automobile cemetery: all decomposing in the damp, pestilential air, like the carcasses of prehistoric monsters. At nightfall, Belmont Park fills up with people. Clandestine encounters, following a furtive glance, a flick of the hand, and couples disappear into nearby hotels. Jack is seated at an outdoor table. A hunchback appears with an accordion and, staggering drunkenly, begins to play, but the notes are so harsh and false that the crowd boos and obliges him to move on. Silence. People gazing into space. In a booth, a woman in sunglasses is selling lottery tickets, but no-one is buying. Jack returns to the projection booth. On the screen, a regiment of armed marines circles a square, the only sound the squeaking of crêpe soles on asphalt. Suddenly, Jack realizes that his lips are moving, shaping words that he hasn't chosen, the meaning of which escapes him: inarticulate sounds, interminable phrases that could never mean anything to anyone. He moves back down Boulevard Gouin, sensing that he must put an end to his investigation: too many films, too many faces, too many wars jostling one another in his brain. He's suffering from cinematic indigestion. The passers-by, the mannequins in the store windows, the neon signs, all are as unreal as figures in a dream. A comet darts across the night sky, and in the light of its passage he distinguishes Bernard, Erik the Viking, Jolin. The comet accelerates and he realizes that it is his head spinning out there in the darkness, dragging in its wake all the films he has ever seen. Any moment now, it will explode and he will find himself back in the street, suffering from a loss of memory, unable to find his way back to the Commodore, lost in a celluloid labyrinth.

VI

Later , the text will be born, the vapour condensing on it under the refrigerating effect of syntax and plot. For the moment, the words pass by very quickly, vague, formless, the result of the imposed delay. Jack must finish the story he is writing in the Commodore's projection booth during the showing of this film, must use a pen to outrace the unwinding of the reels; otherwise, the manuscript will cease to exist, he will burn it at the end of this double feature, which fortunately is four hours long. It's not a matter of taking the shortest and easiest route, it's a matter simply of forging ahead, gaining the upper hand of the brief epileptic seizures that invalidate sight and sound.

Later, when the spectators file out of the hall, their bodies numb and their eyes glassy, as if they had just awakened from a long sleep, Jack may consign these sheets piling up on his right to oblivion. He recalls how his encounter with Jolin insidiously involved him in an investigation of the tenuous, almost invisible thread connecting events sometimes occurring at intervals of more than a thousand years: explosive dispersion in time, highly dangerous. But the state of verbal emergency that he himself has decreed prevents him from going back on his choice, this particular story being the only one to interest him to the point of obsession. A story so lacking in continuity that he repeatedly runs the risk of losing himself in it, never knowing when he will appear himself as a character, his words and actions ordained by the logic of the narration.

VII

At the top of the hill, before the antique dealer's house, Jack turns into a dirt drive. He parks in the farmyard, behind a Volkswagen van riddled with rust. He enters the kitchen without knocking. Julie is hanging from a rope wound about the centre beam. She hasn't used a slip knot, so the noose grips her neck only at the level of the larynx. Two or three minutes more, and she'll be dead. A number of people are scattered about the unfurnished room, leaning against the walls, listening to a scratchy record that keeps repeating the same guitar chords over and over and smoking acrid-smelling cigarettes. Jack seizes Julie about the waist and lifts her back onto the vegetable crate from which she has leapt.

A man approaches, smiling blissfully, and presses with all his weight on Julie's shoulders. Jack strikes him in the face. While he crawls about on the floor, searching for his glasses, the frames of which have broken, Jack succeeds in cutting Julie down. She coughs and rubs her neck. The only light in the room comes from a television set sitting on the floor, its screen filled momentarily with the distorted, flickering images of a western film. "I'll have your hide, Billy!" Jack pushes

Julie outside. She sits on the edge of the well, which is covered with a sheet of plywood. The mountains stand massed against the darkening sky. The engine of the car is still idling. Jack turns the lights on high. Hundreds of mosquitoes flit about the double beams. Shielding her eyes, Julie says in a hoarse voice:

"It was only a game, they would have cut me down in time."

"Who are they?"

"My colleagues in the archaeological society. We've finished our digging for the summer. . . . How did you find me?"

"Jolin told me you'd be spending a few days here. Maybe he's bugged your place, too."

Someone has raised the volume of the television set. A horse whinnies, there are gunshots.

"He didn't need any bugging equipment to know we were coming here," says Julie. "This is his farm. He invited us here to watch Bernard and his crew begin shooting on his film."

"My brother? But that doesn't make any sense."

Jack recalls the report he received this morning from the investigator, according to which Bernard died accidentally in a tunnel under construction. The detective provided no evidence to support this conclusion, only a bill for services rendered. Perhaps that was his way of trying to make his client pay up.

Jack hears someone whistling behind the house. He places an arm about Julie's waist and leads her in the direction of the barn, which has not housed any animals for a long time. Suddenly, on their left, there is a burst of light: an arrangement of neon tubes on the wall of the barn has just flicked on. Jack recognizes what the darkness was concealing: the white façade of a building with a false slatted roof, movie posters, a lighted sign with the name COMMODORE written on it. It's a rough copy of his own movie house, using the barn as a backdrop. Denis emerges from the building, still whistling, unrolling an electric wire. He waves to Jack.

"You've arrived just in time," he says.

"For what?"

"The big boom!"

Watching Denis attach his wire to a detonator, Jack suddenly understands what is going on.

"I've checked the place carefully," says Denis. There's no-one in there. But you should warn the others up at the farmhouse to keep their distance."

"There's no danger," replies Julie. "They won't stir out of that house."

Denis shrugs and glances at his watch.

"Two minutes to go."

Jack asks him what the mock Commodore looks like inside.

"Just an empty barn," replies Denis with a smile.

The poster on the left depicts a savage-looking man standing before a drakkar, wielding an axe; the one on the right, a tyrannosaurus crushing an American Army tank in its jaws.

"Is no-one going to film the explosion?" asks Jack.

"I don't know. Jolin told me your brother has placed his cameras far back on that hill over there. From that distance, the imperfections in the set won't be noticeable."

"That's pure nonsense," says Jack, raising his voice. "Like all the rest of his stories. If Bernard were around, he'd come and speak to us. Why should he hide to film the script?"

In the silence that follows, Jack has the acute impression that he is being watched. He looks quickly about him; his eyes encounter nothing but the night. He finds himself imagining the improbable case of a projector that would emit darkness instead of light; one which, instead of illuminating a screen, would cast its white surface into shadow, but so rapidly that the eye would be unable to record the pulsation. And what would such an imaginary movie house resemble, if not those sheets that Jack covered with writing and left in the projection booth of the Commodore? But which Commodore? This fictitious one, or the real one back in Cartierville? And as Denis pushes them down behind the tractor, the sound of the detonation filling their ears before reverberating off the nearby mountains, he understands what this demolition corresponds to in Jolin's mind. The archaeologists come running from the house. Jack recognizes the man he knocked to the floor a short while ago; the broken stem of his glasses has been repaired with adhesive tape.

"You should have told us," the man says to Julie. "We've missed the best part. Where did your friends set up their cameras?"

Julie doesn't reply. And Jack wonders what she sees in that conflagration, which is throwing showers of sparks over the surrounding fields. Perhaps another fire, lit a thousand years before? He watches right to the end as, page by page, Jolin's text is simultaneously burned and written.

VIII

Screens of smoke, dust and fire suddenly rise into the sky on the northern front of the occupied zone. Against this backdrop, a cloud of little black dots rises and falls back: the disjointed bodies of soldiers. The final offensive designed to break the insurgents' resistance has begun. Bernard receives an order from headquarters: all battalions must attempt individually to cross the enemy lines, the rallying centre being a point two miles west of the besieged city. He communicates the command to his unit and, 30 minutes later, the exhausted, bedraggled men assemble on the grounds of City Hall. But they refuse to obey the order, reluctant to leave this terrain they have been defending since the onset of winter. So Bernard resigns himself to awaiting the arrival of the enemy, standing with his men, his gaze fixed on an indeterminate point in the distance.